THE GIRL IS MINE

By

EMMA EHI

MAPLE
PUBLISHERS

The Girl is Mine

Author: EMMA EHI

Copyright © 2024 EMMA EHI

The right of EMMA EHI to be identified as author of this work has been asserted by the author in accordance with section 77 and 78 of the Copyright, Designs and Patents Act 1988.

First Published in 2024

ISBN 978-1-83538-153-3 (Paperback)
     978-1-83538-154-0 (Hardback)
     978-1-83538-155-7 (E-Book)

Book Cover Design and Book Layout by:
     White Magic Studios
     www.whitemagicstudios.co.uk

Published by:
     Maple Publishers
     Fairbourne Drive, Atterbury,
     Milton Keynes,
     MK10 9RG, UK
     www.maplepublishers.com

CONTENTS

Chapter 1 – The Hexenburg School of Witchcraft......5

Chapter 2 – The Last Element 21

Chapter 3 – Nogokpo........................... 49

Chapter 4 – The Send-Off Party 75

Chapter 5 – The Mission 92

Chapter 6 – Jenny, Where Are You? 118

Chapter 7 – The Confrontation 137

Chapter 8 – The Showdown 150

Foreword

In much of the Western world today, witches and wizards exist only in legends. But throughout Africa and some parts of the same Western world, the notion of witch-craft is very real. The spirit world is no less present than the physical world and those who can harness its powers to harm are generally feared.

Ironically, in the past, it was thought that development, urbanization, modernization, education or the adoption of major religions like Christianity or Islam would lead to the disappearance of beliefs and practices related to witchcraft. But far from fading away, witchcraft is no longer limited to the domain of the secret or unspoken, it is present in daily life. In many parts of Africa,

Although, in many climes, few would say witchcraft does not exist; However, beliefs in witchcraft are deep-seated and widespread. In many parts of Africa, it is generally believed that witches and wizards have no control over their actions and only use their powers to do harm and destroy and there is a strong psychological fear of witches among people.

Remarkably, in many places where people profess Christianity or Islam, a majority tends to dread juju, voodoo and traditional practices and show more faith in that direction – Many criminals and politicians would rather swear with the holy books in their hands than swear before a shrine.

Emma Ehi

Chapter 1

The Hexenburg School of Witchcraft

Jenny turned on her music box with the timer and carefully placed it on the table in the sitting room. Soon, the pair of little human sculptures, one male and one female, began dancing and twirling around on the flat surface of the vase. Jenny's lips curled with amusement as she and her father watched the figurines whirl to the gentle, programmed tune emanating from the box.

Suddenly, while the little dancing show was ongoing, Dieter, Jenny's father, who seemed to be enjoying the show, reached for the female partner of the dancing sculptures and snatched her from the vase.

"Oh, papa, please, put her back in place!" Jenny pleaded.

"No, I will not put her back in place; I don't want her to dance," replied Dieter.

"Papa, please!" said Jenny, stamping her foot.

But despite Jenny's pleas, her father refused to return the toy. Instead, he stood up and went behind the sofa, initiating a playful chase. Jenny, seeing it as their usual game, joined in and tried to retrieve the little female sculpture.

After some playful running around, Dieter ran outside onto the streets, still holding the toy in his hands. However, determined to get her toy back, Jenny ran after him.

"Papa, papa, please, give it back to me!" she implored. As Jenny chased after her father, she accidentally fell into a gully.

"Jenny! Jenny!" Dieter called out, searching the gully, but there was no response. Jenny had mysteriously disappeared from his sight.

Meanwhile, Jenny was awakened in her room by her mother's voice intruding into her dreams.

"You were talking in your sleep - you must have been dreaming," said Petra.

While Dieter was groping around the mouth of the gully searching and calling out to his daughter, at that very moment a mellow and more distinct voice was at the same time calling out to Jenny, who was all this while sleeping in her room. Jenny! Jenny! Are you still sleeping?" said Petra softly - The sound of her mother's voice had suddenly intruded into her dreams.

"You were talking in your sleep - you must have been dreaming." said Petra.

Jenny sat up and rubbed her eyes. "Good morning, mama," she said, with a dreamy, tired look in her eyes.

"Good morning," Petra responded, her voice gentle and caring. "Did you sleep well?" she asked, her eyes filled with tender affection as she looked at her daughter.

Jenny nodded with a small smile. "Papa took my doll and refused to give it back!" Jenny exclaimed, her frustration evident.

"Oh, really?" Petra responded with a sympathetic tone.

"Yes, mama. I kept pleading with him to give it back, but he refused," Jenny explained.

"Don't worry, you know your father loves and cares about you," Petra reassured Jenny, her words soothing.

"You slept too long; You're going to be late to school. Go prepare yourself, while I get the food ready," Petra added, seamlessly transitioning to her next task as she left the room with a sense of calm authority.

"Okay, mam," replied Jenny, jumping out of the bed, and drawing back the window curtains before packing and wrapping her long hair in a bob at the top.

Jenny was a vivacious and pretty young girl who had a happy family and a lot of admirers. Everyone doted on the fair-haired beauty whose doll-like eyes always had a twinkle. She and her younger brother, Kai who, just like Jenny, was still at school, were surrounded by love and affection from their parents and they were a huge source of joy and pride for the family.

Jenny's father, Dieter, was a sprightly and cheerful man who worked as a horse breeder. He had a large stud farm where pigs and chickens were kept. He worked part-time as a beekeeper, too. He kept bees, housing them in hives in the farmland and extracting and jarring the honey in the shed at the back of his house.

Petra, Jenny's mother, taught in the school of witches in Hexenburg, a quiet, northern German town known for its fresh fishes, seafood, and clear blue sky.

After the family had breakfasted that morning, Petra dropped Jenny off in her school and then, drove straight to work. Dropping her daughter off to school was now a daily routine for the witch.

On arrival at the Hexenburg school where she worked, Petra briefly popped into Ursula's office to see if all was well. Ursula was the school's director. It was a Monday, the first working day of the week and Petra wanted to find out how the director had spent her weekend. After some light-hearted chat with Ursula and some members of the staff of the school, the teacher went to meet her students in the class.

Petra had been teaching in the school for more than two years. Her duty was to train the young students in the mysterious world of witchcraft, and she took great pride in her work. She began her career working as a cashier in one of the local train stations in Hexenburg, but she hated the dreariness of the job coupled with the fact that she always had to leave very early in the morning and drive long distances as part of her job.

After a few years on the job, she then had a brief spell working in the Hexenburg Circus where she showcased her skills doing tricks to entertain the people. Her experience working as an illusionist taught her many valuable lessons. Still not satisfied with her professional life, Petra decided to become a witch and subsequently obtained some training in witchcraft in Hamburg, where she had the privilege of being exposed to the inner intricacies of the craft. After getting a teaching job in the renowned Hexenburg School of Witches, she felt she was, at last, living her dream.

Petra was a creative, hardworking, and charismatic woman and, like all truly charismatic people, she could work her magic on both men and women and had a magic touch with the children, too. Ursula, her boss, had on several occasions commended her work ethics and genius at organizing people.

On arrival at the Hexenburg school where she worked, Petra briefly popped into Ursula's office to see if all was well. Ursula, the school's director, held a position of authority and responsibility. As Monday dawned, Petra, curious about how Ursula had spent her weekend, sought her out. Ursula's excitement was palpable as she shared news of the upcoming global conference of witches and wizards scheduled to take place in Nigeria. She revealed to Petra that she had been chosen as one of the representatives from Germany, a responsibility that filled her with pride and anticipation. After some light-hearted chat with Ursula and some members of the staff of the school, the teacher went to meet her students in the class.

Petra had been teaching in the school for more than two years. Her duty was to train the young students in the mysterious world of witchcraft, and she took great pride in her work. She began her career working as a cashier in one of the local train stations in Hexenburg, but she hated the dreariness of the job coupled with the fact that she always had to leave very early in the morning and drive long distances as part of her job.

After a few years on the job, she then had a brief spell working in the Hexenburg Circus where she showcased her skills doing tricks to entertain people. Her experience working as an illusionist taught her many valuable lessons.

Still not satisfied with her professional life, Petra decided to become a witch and subsequently obtained some training in witchcraft in Hamburg, where she had the privilege of being exposed to the inner intricacies of the craft. After getting a teaching job in the renowned Hexenburg School of Witches, she felt she was finally living her dream.

Petra greeted her students with a warm smile as she entered the classroom.

"Good morning, Mrs. Petra," the pupils chorused in response.

After dropping her bag on the table in front of the class and settling down, the teacher asked the class what they had learned the previous week. Many eager hands shot up, and she called on Stefan to answer.

"Last week, we learned how to move objects with the aid of a magic wand without touching them," Stefan answered.

"Good!" Petra praised. "And who can demonstrate that to the class?" asked the teacher.

Most of the pupils raised their hands. "Melanie." said the teacher. Melanie sprang to her feet, took her magic wand, and went in front of the class. The teacher placed some coins beside a glass saucer on the table.

Melanie stepped forward and stretched her magic wand towards one of the coins. "Vom treffpunkt aus zwei parallelen linien, Ete, Beta, ich flehe auch an - Verzaubern!" She recited the spell. Without any physical contact, Melanie tried to magically move the coins from the table into the saucer. She succeeded after her third trial, using her powers of concentration, as her young eyes zeroed in on the coins, picking them up one after the other and successfully placing them in the open saucer with the aid of her magic wand.

After that, a few of the other pupils were asked to show their magical abilities of moving small objects on the table without touching them. When the teacher was satisfied the young students were good enough at the given tasks, she decided to move on to the next lesson: „The vanishing cream." She explained how to make and use the special cream that could make people invisible.

"Open your course books to chapter four," said the teacher. "The topic of our lesson today is, 'The vanishing cream.' We're going to learn how to make and use the special cream that can make people invisible," continued the teacher.

The pupils were subsequently taught how to make and apply the vanishing cream which was also called the invisible ink. Stephan and Christian were called to the front of the class to demonstrate the cream's power. Stephan stood behind Christian, placing his hands on the latter's shoulder; He was asked to keep tapping his shoulder. Then, Sabina applied the cream on Stephan, causing parts of his body to disappear, much to the amazement of the class.

Bit by bit, piece by piece, with every stroke of Sabina's brush while applying the cream, the physical presence of Stephan's body was instantaneously erased in real time and preternaturally transplanted into the state of invisibility. Only a pair of bodiless hands tapping on Christian's shoulders could be seen - A pair of hands that did not encounter the invisible ink. After that, the process was reversed and his invisible body became visible, once again. The exercise was an interesting transcendental experience for the pupils, more so for young Stephan. After the session, the astonished aspiring young witches and wizards were taught how to produce the special cream.

Meanwhile, on the field, another group of students were being given practical lessons on flying with the aid of a magical broom. For most of the students, this was one of the most eagerly anticipated lessons. Their teacher, Mathias, could hear the excitement in the enthusiastic young students' voices and while some of them felt a twinge of nervousness at the task of flying on a broom, the eyes of the others twinkled with merriment as they were taught and guided on their broom-flying exercises.

The students cheered whenever one of them took their turn to fly. They were all very keen to learn and demonstrate their flying skills and the young witches and wizards glowed with pride whenever they successfully performed the not-so-easy task which they were made to go through progressively without rush to prevent injuries from any fall. On the first day, not many of the pupils were able to complete the task; However, in subsequent exercises, the patient tutor was able to guide most of the class to fly on their own without guidance.

The students were back in school on the first school day of the following week. That was the day a very special guest who was a magician was visiting the school. The news of the magician's proposed visit was music to the ears of the young students at the school who were all looking forward to it. The visitor was 'the wise old bird,' named Karl-Heinz, the highly respected sorcerer and famous magician of Hexenburg

After their regular lessons in the morning, while the youngsters were waiting for their August visitor, one of them asked their teacher, Petra, to sing them a song. The teacher readily obliged. She cleared her voice and began to sing one of her favourite songs she learnt as a kid:

"When Melanie was a little girl.

Her parents asked her, saying,

'Melanie, what would you like to be when you grow up?'

'Papa, mama,' replied little Melanie.

'When I grow up, I'd like to be a witch.

So, I could have supernatural powers!'

'Oh, no, no, my daughter!' said her mother,

'Witchcraft is not a profession.

Some witches are condemned in many nations.

But you could study a normal profession,

In a good higher institution.'

'My daughter,' said her father.

'You could study law.

You could study Medicine.

You could study Engineering.

Or you could study business.

But not witchcraft,

To have supernatural powers!'

'So, now, Melanie, tell me, 'Said her mother,

'What would you like to be when you grow up?'

'Mama, papa,' replied little Melanie,

'When I grow up, I'd like to be a witch.

So, I could have magic powers!'

Hardly had the teacher finished her song when Ursula, the school's director, entered the classroom, her presence commanding attention. Behind her followed Karl-Heinz, the sorcerer and magician, with his distinguished long, flowing white beard.

Ursula, affectionately known as Ushi or Ulla by her colleagues and admirers, exuded warmth, and brilliance. Her quiet authority and sharp intelligence earned her widespread admiration and reverence. Her dynamic leadership played a significant role in the school's renowned reputation, inspiring all who crossed its threshold.

From a young age, Ursula's fascination with witchcraft blossomed, laying the foundation for her lifelong passion. Her early immersion in the craft profoundly shaped her future, equipping her with the fundamental knowledge needed to realize her dreams.

As a child, Ursula's curiosity knew no bounds, and she viewed the world as her playground. Whether venturing into the woods with friends or engaging in imaginative play in her father's backyard, she embraced every opportunity for exploration and discovery. From games of "Kill the Bad Witch with the Arrow" to fanciful adventures in Uncle Jurgen's backyard, Ursula's childhood experiences fuelled her imagination and set her on a path towards embracing the mystical world of witchcraft.

She always had a secret wish - if she was going to be a pro at something, that special something was to be a witch. Fortunately, she had the work ethic to get there, and she believed she could succeed at whatever she wanted to do if she put her mind to it and worked hard enough. She had no burdens in front of her and no impediments to her ambitions. She was from a family that bore an honoured name in Hexenburg and by choosing to be a witch, she was following in the footsteps of her father, who was a wizard; as well as her grandfather, who was a sorcerer. She learned a lot from her father, who was widely respected for his craft and whose work directly touched the lives of many in Hexenburg and beyond. Sometimes, Ursula would accompany him to the coven in Hamburg where the great witches and wizards in the region used to meet. Years later, after the death of her father, she founded the Hexenburg School of witches. The illustrious school director's work had been largely limited to Hexenburg, but she could not be disregarded in Germany and her experience and contribution to her craft shone through the field of renowned witches and wizards who populate the German and European space.

"Good morning, class!" said Ursula, smilingly.

"Good morning, Mrs. Ursula!" replied the young students.

"I'd like to introduce to you our very special guest today, Mr. Karl-Heinz. He will be entertaining you, today. He will also be revealing to you some deep, deep secrets," said the director.

Karl-Heinz was Ursula's good friend and colleague. Confident and respectable, he was a wise and virtuous man who was well-grounded in sorcery and one who had brought a different dimension to witchcraft in Germany.

"Good morning," said Karl-Heinz to the class.

"Good morning, Mr. Karl-Heinz!" answered the young students, who were excited to see him.

"I've been informed how brilliant you all are, and I'm truly encouraged and happy to be here." said the soft-spoken sorcerer. "Today, I'm going to show you something special," he continued.

The young students sat on the edge of their seats, their eyes wide with wonder and anticipation, as the magician began his performance. With a flick of his wand and a whispered incantation, he delved into a mesmerizing display of spells and illusions.

First, he produced a deck of cards seemingly out of thin air, manipulating them with precision and grace as they danced between his nimble fingers. Then, with a flourish, he made a bunch of flowers bloom from his empty hands, filling the air with their sweet fragrance.

As the magician continued his enchanting spectacle, he levitated objects effortlessly and transformed them before their very eyes. Coins disappeared and reappeared in mysterious places, and ordinary handkerchiefs were transformed into fluttering butterflies. The young students were spellbound and captivated as the magician unveiled his dazzling array of tricks. With every flourish and sleight of hand, he commanded their attention, earning resounding cheers and applause from the budding sorcerers and enchantresses in the room.

After entertaining them with a display of magic in the classroom, they all subsequently went to the school's swimming pool where the sorcerer gave the students a lesson on levitation. To demonstrate his powers, the magician shot his eyes and stood still for a while beside the pool of water. He remained motionless for a while before uttered some magic words, and then, he slowly rose from the ground and began floating above the water without any physical support.

After floating in mid-air for a while, Karl-Heinz started walking back and forth above the water with his feet above the highest point of the water in the pool. A great cheer went up from the crowd. The magician returned the cheers by nodding and giving a warm glowing smile. Even though they were witches and wizards themselves, however, Karl-Heinz's magical tricks and gravity-defying moves re-ignited their sense of wonder.

"Wow, that's all very impressive!" said Petra.

"Truly amazing stuff!" Mathias remarked.

"Karl is a transcendent genius of a wizard and one of the pearls of our realm," said Ursula. Then she continued, "Sometimes, when he does certain things, one has the impression he's not there, that he's hiding, but he's there and everyone knows it."

"The good thing about him is his humility and great sense of humour," said Mathias.

"Oh, yes!" concurred Ursula. "Each day, Karl wakes up and looks for the affection of his people. I like the love he has for his craft," revealed the director.

"He's the gentlest of wizards and one who also enjoys a drink and a bit of jokes," added Petra.

A few months later, the school had a break. Petra had been working so hard and thought she needed some rest. The following weekend, the family was relaxing in the sitting room which was prettily furnished. Two little figures of a witch and a wizard hung from the roof.

"I'd like to take a trip somewhere and have a complete change of environment," Petra suddenly announced.

"Oh, that would be great! A change of environment would do you some good!" replied Dieter. "And where would you like to visit?" he asked.

"Oh... I don't know. Maybe, the United States or the Caribbean, or maybe a visit to Africa," replied Petra.

"Mam, since you've not made up your mind where you'd like to go, let's draw lots on the countries and decide your destination by a game of chance," suggested Jenny.

"That sounds good, why not?" replied Petra.

Jenny ran inside and returned with a globe which she placed on the table.

"Mam, I'm going to spin the globe around and all you've got to do is to stop it from spinning with the tip of your finger - We can then choose from the nearest continent or country to your point of contact with the globe, okay?" said Jenny.

"Okay, baby, let's go!" answered Petra.

Jenny then set the globe spinning and her mother stopped the spinning globe with the tip of her finger. Her point of contact with the rotating globe was an area showing the African continent.

"Africa!" Jenny and Dieter chorused.

"But, where exactly in Africa?" asked Dieter.

"Wait!" replied Jenny, as she walked across the room and picked up a map that was lying on a little stool beside the television set.

"Okay, here's a map of Africa," said Jenny, unfolding the map and spreading it out on the table. She reached for some pins from a little glass jar and pinned the map to the wall.

"Mam, I 'm going to blindfold you and all you have to do is to touch any country on the map with this pen," said Jenny.

She took a scarf and lightly tied her mother's eyes with it so that the latter could not see. Jenny gave Petra a pen. "Alright, mam it's up to you," said Jenny.

Jenny took her mother's hand and led her towards the map on the wall. On getting close, Petra stretched her hand and touched the map on the wall with the pen. Jenny took off the blindfold around her mother's eyes without her taking the tip of the pen off the wall.

"Nigeria!" said Jenny.

"So, your destination is Nigeria," said Dieter.

"Uhmm, yes, but that's very strange!" Said Petra. "Incidentally, Nigeria is the place where the first-ever global conference of witches will be held, soon, and I 've been selected as one of the participants." She disclosed.

"Really? But you never mentioned that to me. That's great!" Dieter exclaimed. "But why are you looking worried?" He asked.

"It looks like I'd be visiting Nigeria twice this year; Moreover, I don't know much about Nigeria," replied Petra. "Tomorrow, I shall visit the tourist firm to arrange for a visa and get some travel brochures about the country," said Petra. "Jenny, would you like to visit Africa with me?" she asked.

"Oh, yes! yes," replied Jenny, looking at her mother with a sparkle of excitement in her eyes. Her eyes got wide as she added enthusiastically, "I would very much love to make my first trip to Africa with you, Mama."

A few days later, the family began preparing for their trip, excited for the adventures that awaited them beyond the familiar surroundings of Hexenburg. The birds were chirping and twittering from the branches of the low tree outside her window and their beautiful singing voices had woken Jenny up earlier than usual. She stood up from her bed and drew back the window curtains and looked outside - it was a bright and beautiful day. She was ecstatic at the prospect of travelling with her mother to Nigeria. Suddenly, the alarm clock went off; She had set it for seven o'clock, but she was already awake before this time, perhaps due to her excitement.

She grabbed the clock and turned off the alarm and momentarily caught sight of a radiantly smiling picture of her that was hanging on the wall, as she looked around her cozy, moderately decorated room whose walls were painted in cheerful colours. She needed to check her messages but couldn't find her mobile phone. Just then, it occurred to her that she'd forgotten it in her mother's room the night before.

Petra was already up and working in the kitchen. The day before, she had already prepared everything they would need for their trip. After seeing her mother briefly in the kitchen, Jenny, who had her hair bunched up on her head in a thick luxurious mass, went to take her bath. Moments later, she planted herself in front of the mirror; she let her hair drop and the very long loose luxuriant bunch cascaded down her back in a flourish.

She twisted around in front of the mirror as she combed her hair that was her crowning glory. She felt bright and full of energy. Her blithe and cheerful nature were some of the qualities her numerous friends admired about her, and she was the remarkable and enduring blue-eyed girl everyone had grown to love.

When she was done with the make-up of her hair, Jenny went into her room and re-emerged clutching a pile of clothes, she was unable to decide what dress to put on.

"Mam, what do you think of this dress I've got on, is it okay?" she asked her mother.

"No, I think you look best in the other one; I mean, the one you had on the first time," replied Petra.

As the family packed their bags and prepared for their trip to Africa, they couldn't help but feel excited about the adventures that awaited them beyond the familiar surroundings of Hexenburg and hoped their adventures in Africa would bring them closer together, strengthening their bonds and opening their eyes to the wonders of the world beyond their home town.

With Petra's desire for a change of environment and the anticipation of exploring new cultures and landscapes, they set off on their journey, ready to embrace the unknown and create unforgettable memories together. Shortly after, mother and daughter were on their way to the airport to catch their flight to Lagos.

Chapter 2

The Last Element

It has been two weeks when the witches and wizards from across the globe met in Chicago, USA, to announce their historic inaugural universal conference to be held in Africa. After much deliberation, the general assembly of the council unanimously chose the vibrant City of Benin in Nigeria as their venue, and setting the date for less than three months away....

News of the upcoming conference quickly spread throughout the ancient Benin City, capturing the attention of its residents, and sparking a mix of excitement and scepticism. Among those taken aback by the announcement was Archbishop Idaho, a prominent figure in the city known for his strong beliefs.

Upon hearing the news, Archbishop Idaho was quick to express disbelief, declaring, "It's not true!" However, as speculation continued to swirl, the press sought out his opinion on the matter. When questioned about the potential consequences if the conference were indeed to take place, the archbishop remained steadfast in his scepticism, yet contemplative about the potential implications for the community.

"Witches from around the world could not come to Benin because I would kill them all!" The archbishop declared.

Following Archbishop Idaho's initial disbelief regarding the proposed world conference, the press wasted no time in relaying his sentiments to the chief host of the event who, incidentally, was also living in the city where the conference was scheduled to take place. Upon hearing Idaho's scepticism, Eboho, the chief host, responded assertively, stating, "Not even God can stop it. I am a wizard and I know the power that we carry."

Undeterred by Idaho's doubts, the press returned to the archbishop's residence to inform him of Eboho's confident declaration.

"Indeed, he is correct," responded the clergyman, causing a stir among the gathered press, who eagerly awaited the unfolding of this unexpected twist.

"He is correct?" they queried, seeking clarification.

"God does not need to concern Himself with matters as trivial as halting a conference of witches. That is why I am here," declared Archbishop Idaho, viewing this challenge as an opportunity to strengthen his faith. The archbishop then inquired about the expected attendance at the conference, to which the press revealed a staggering figure of 9,800 witches and wizards.

Meanwhile, the leaders of the African witches and wizards closely monitored the developments through televised coverage. Their appointed conference host, Eboho, took to the airwaves, boldly proclaiming to the world that nothing would deter or prevent the upcoming conference.

The media representatives approached Idaho at his residence, expressing their concerns about the risks he was taking.

"Archbishop, you're treading on thin ice," they warned. The clergyman raised an eyebrow. "What's that supposed to mean?" he inquired.

"You need to tread carefully," they advised.

"Those who tread carefully seldom make a mark, and those who make a mark seldom tread carefully," Idaho retorted with conviction.

"Are you willing to address the nation on camera and convey your message to us, so we can relay it to Eboho?" a reporter asked.

"Bring it on!" Idaho replied confidently, ready to face any challenge head-on.

A few days later, both Archbishop Idaho and Eboho found themselves seated in the TV studio, facing each other and the cameras. The atmosphere was tense, with anticipation hanging thick in the air as viewers tuned in to witness this pivotal moment unfold.

"I don't want anyone to die among you," said the anchor man, "are you really sure you are bringing 9,800 witches and wizards from all over the world?" He asked.

"Yes." Replied Eboho.

The moderator turned to the archbishop, seeking clarification: "Dr. Idaho, are you absolutely certain you'll put an end to the meeting?"

"I'm not just planning to stop it; it's already stopped," Idaho declared firmly.

The anchor then addressed both men, proposing a debate: "Gentlemen, I'm granting you one hour to showcase the strength of your beliefs. Eboho, are you up for it?"

"Absolutely," Eboho agreed.

"But before we conclude, I'll have a prayer," Idaho interjected, fixing his gaze directly on Eboho. The statement carried an undeniable weight, hinting at a deeper confrontation to come.

"Fine," Eboho responded calmly, his demeanour poised despite the tension crackling in the studio. However, the Clergyman's retort cut through the air like a blade, his words laced with an eerie resolve as he stared directly into his opponent's eyes.

As the cameras rolled, Eboho addressed the audience, his voice steady as he expounded on the strength of witches and wizards, drawing parallels from ancient texts and magical lore. The moderator, turning to Idaho, sought his response to Eboho's assertions, "Did you hear him?" He asked.

"Yes," Idaho replied simply, his gaze unwavering.

"And what do you have to say in return?" Inquired the host.

"I have nothing to say; the meeting is cancelled," Idaho declared firmly, his tone brooking no argument.

"Why?" Asked the anchor, taken aback.

"No divination spell, no incantation spell shall stand in the presence of the righteous," Idaho proclaimed, citing passages from the Bible to support his stance. Then, fixing his gaze on Eboho, he issued a chilling ultimatum. "It's time for me to kill this man. If I truly serve the divine, let fire descend from the heavens. Answer me honestly: Are you a witch?"

The studio buzzed with tension as the audience held their breath. "Just say yes or no," Idaho demanded, his voice commanding attention. "If you say yes, I'll act accordingly. Are you a witch?"

"No," Eboho replied, his voice steady but laced with an undercurrent of uncertainty.

"Then leave!" thundered Idaho, his words resonating with authority. The confrontation ended as swiftly as it began, leaving a palpable sense of relief mingled with disbelief in its wake.

The following morning, Eboho made a covert visit to Idaho's office, quietly slipping in to borrow a Bible. Meanwhile, the media swarmed Eboho's residence later in the day, eager to ascertain whether the highly anticipated global witches' meeting would proceed as planned.

"Oh, yes!" Eboho affirmed without hesitation, his stance unwavering despite the mounting pressure.

"If the meeting does happen, mark my words—I will burn this Bible!" thundered Idaho from his residence, his voice resolute with conviction, after being told what Eboho said to the press.

The African witches and wizards, observing the events unfold, couldn't hide their disappointment at Eboho's apparent surrender on live television. "How can one man calling himself an archbishop halt an international conference? We shall see." Sabon Gari, one of the high-ranking wizards muttered, his frustration palpable – Those who knew Sabon Sabon, as he was popularly called in the coven, knew he never played on a losing team.

In the days leading up to the scheduled global gathering, just as anticipation reached its peak, Idaho made a pivotal visit to the Nigerian Head of State, seeking to ensure that his decree against the conference held firm.

"I have made it clear to the entire nation: there will be no assembly of witches and wizards," Idaho reiterated to the country's leader.

"On the day of your televised declaration, I immediately dispatched communications to all embassies worldwide, barring any wizard from setting foot in Nigeria," the Nigerian Head of State affirmed. Upon learning of this decisive action from the country's leader, the witches and wizards found their hopes dashed, and left disheartened by the unforeseen turn of events.

It was just past 5am, and the early morning hustle and bustle of Lagos were beginning to stir. In the Lawanson Community of Surulere, life was slowly awakening, with activity starting to buzz.

At the motor park, a commercial bus driver was taking a moment to relax in his vehicle, enjoying a sip of cola while Afro juju music played from his stationary bus's sound system. His conductor perched on the edge of the old, weather-beaten bus, popularly called 'molue', calling out destinations, "Orile! Straight to Orile! Eko Idumota!" in a loud, husky voice, competing with other conductors to attract passengers.

Meanwhile, on the rooftop of a nearby building, a bird patiently waited for its partner, observing the bustling scene below. Finally, it spotted its feathered companion flying towards it, darting between buildings at the opposite end of the road. However, in its attempt to navigate through the maze of overhead electric cables, the bird misjudged the distance and became entangled in the wires - which was strange, as birds do not normally get caught in such entanglements.

Nearly fifteen minutes later, when the electricity was restored, the unfortunate bird was electrocuted. The lone bird hovered briefly, then settled on a nearby rooftop, chirping softly to communicate with its partner. Moments later, the electrocuted bird transformed, changing from bird to human form, still suspended among the tangled wires.

With no response from her partner, the woman flew closer to the ground and transformed completely into human form. Misty-eyed and concerned for her partner's well-being, she lamented the possibility of his demise, unable to reach him with her calls.

"Kunle! Kunle! Are you okay?" she called out repeatedly, her voice filled with worry as she scanned the area, desperate for any sign of life from her partner. With each passing moment, her concern grew, unsure of what to do next.

In the bustling streets of Surulere, community members had formed Civil Defence groups, dedicated to keeping their neighbourhood safe. Every night, these vigilant groups of young men patrolled the area, keeping a watchful eye out for any signs of trouble or danger.

On this morning, two members of one of these local groups were heading home after a night of patrolling. As they passed by, they noticed the woman, frantically trying to communicate with what appeared to be a person suspended between the high-tension cables.

"Wh - wh - what's that man do - do - doing on the pole?" one of the young men who had speech impediment asked curiously, jerking his head, and swinging his arms while battling to utter his words.

The two walked closer to the woman to have a better view. "Ah, the man is dead-o!" cried the other young man. They walked closer to the middle-aged woman.

"I - I - I saw - saw you sp - sp - speaking with him ju - ju - just now, do - do you know him?" the stuttering young man inquired, blinking his eyes, and simultaneously tapping his knee to let the words out.

"Ehm ... I don't know him." replied the woman.

"But I - I - sa - sa - saw you l-l-loo looking upwards and sp-speaking with him." The man stuttered. "L-l-let me ask you once again, do - do - do you know him?" He barked, further tapping his knee, and stamping his foot, but this time with more difficulties speaking.

"Ehm, yes, he is my friend," replied the woman.

"Where are you coming from and why is your partner up there?" asked the other man.

"We were returning home when he got stuck there." answered the shivering woman.

"Returning home from where? Speak fast and tell us everything, otherwise, we'll strike you down, now!" the man threatened. The woman refused to speak. Subsequently, the two young men apprehended her.

"Everybody come, come and see a witch!" one of the young men raised an alarm that attracted curious bystanders and residents, some temporarily breaking off whatever they were doing and grabbing their brooms before hurrying to the scene. Soon, a crowd had gathered. As far as they could tell, the man hanging in between the live cables was dead - Nobody could survive in that position. The fire service was called to the scene by one of the residents while the stunned crowd of curious onlookers questioned the woman and threatened to kill her if she didn't open up.

"Please, don't kill me!" she entreated.

"What is your name?" asked one of the men in the crowd.

"Please, I beg you, don't kill me!" she pleaded further.

"Then speak to us and we won't kill you. What's your name?" asked the same young man.

"My name is Meme," replied the woman.

"What's that man doing up there and where are you coming from?" he asked.

"He is my partner, and we were returning home after our activities last night; I don't know what happened because daylight was coming, and we had to get back home quickly." answered Meme.

"You said, 'your activities'? What kind of activities?" asked another man in the crowd.

"Activities with your fellow partners in evil?" cut in another man.

"Ssh, ssh, don't rush her, let her talk." Implored another.

"Now, Meme, or what you call yourself, tell us everything about your activities last night or we will kill you," said the former.

"Please, don't kill me! I will talk!" answered the distraught Meme.

Then, she began to divulge details of their activities from the previous night, along with her surprising history, leaving the crowd utterly bewildered.

"Last night, I cast a cobweb spell on Mama Jonathan's business," the woman confessed, her voice carrying a mix of guilt and defiance.

"What's a cobweb spell?" one curious onlooker inquired, prompting murmurs of agreement from others.

"We communicate with spiders and utilize their webs in our practices. The cobweb spell acts as a form of rejection," Meme explai ned, her tone serious. "It's a complex enchantment that spiritually observes and disorients its target. You may sense the cobweb's presence, but you can't touch it. It signifies abandonment or neglect, causing any good fortune to slip through the affected person's grasp like water through a sieve."

"She is a witch! Let's kill this woman!" screamed one of the broad-chested young men in the crowd.

"No, let her confess," said another. "What else did you do?" he asked.

"Ehm... last night, we urinated and defecated on Chief Owolabi's vehicle, and we made the vehicle's engine break down," said Meme. "Because we have made the engine to be useless, mechanics cannot put it in order even though the vehicle looks new," she continued.

"But why did you decide to attack Chief Owolabi? What has he done to you?" inquired another man in the crowd.

"Ehm... Chief Owolabi cut down the large Cherry tree in his compound where we used to hold our meetings and, worst of all, he's trying to bring electricity to this area, and we don't want that." answered Meme.

"Ehn, you don't want electricity?" asked one of the men in crowd.

"No, we don't want electricity." she replied. "Moreover, Chief Owolabi was becoming too arrogant for my liking. He is always trying to show that he is a big man, so we decided to make his projects to fail by frustrating him to abandon the electricity projects." continued Meme.

Her revelations held the crowd spellbound; disbelief etched on many faces as they absorbed her words. Some members of the Civil Defence group clamoured to mete out their own justice, eager to adhere to their own code of conduct and lynch Meme, their cries of "Kill her! Kill the witch!" echoing through the air. Emotions ran high, curses raining down upon the woman.

"My God, the world is full of mysteries! You'll face punishment for your evil deeds!" exclaimed one horrified bystander.

"This is pure devilry! Such heinous crimes! They're agents of destruction!" shouted another, his voice thick with anger.

It took the intervention of two wise elders to quell the rising tension and rescue Meme from the mob.

"We can't take the law into our own hands by killing this woman," reasoned Pa Akinde, his voice commanding attention. "Now that she's confessed to being a witch, she can no longer stay among us. She must be banished to the village of Nogokpo," he declared.

"Yes, Nogokpo! Send her away!" chorused some of the younger men in agreement.

"These witches are truly wicked!" remarked Olusegun, the second elder. "They obstruct progress, causing harm rather than building. They delight in the suffering of others!" he declared with disdain.

"We don't have witches and wizards in Africa, we have fools!" added Pa Akinde emphatically, nodding in agreement with his fellow elder. "True witches fly to distant lands, achieving great feats. But those who harm others are just foolish. How many children can get scholarships because you fly?" he demanded, fixing Meme with a stern gaze. "Our witches hinder progress instead of contributing to it," he concluded.

"Their deeds are too shameful to speak of openly," continued Pa Akinde. "Like serpentine vampires, they lurk in the shadows by day, emerging under cover of night to prey on the innocent. They can penetrate even the most fortified homes," he added gravely.

With the law offering no recourse for witchcraft accusations, the mob took matters into their own hands, deciding to exile Meme before the authorities arrived. Some of the younger men adorned her with palm fronds and escorted her to the village of Nogokpo, where she would spend the remainder of her days. Though she had lived in Lagos for most of her life, her confession had cost her everything. The locals believed in banishment rather than execution, seeing the witches as unable to control their actions.

Just then, the fire service arrived and brought the impaled lifeless body down from the now de-activated mass of electric cables. At this point, they felt it was of no use rushing him to the hospital for medical attention as they could feel no pulse in his body and thought he could have been dead for a while.

Meanwhile, Jenny and her mother, Petra, arrived safely at the Murtala Mohammed Airport after about a six-hour flight. It was a smooth journey. Sandra, the warm and friendly lady who worked in a tourist firm in the city, was on hand to receive them at the airport and thereafter proceeded straight to their hotel.

"The traffic can be hectic at times, but it is light at this time of the day," said Sandra, when they arrived at the hotel. "You know, Lagos is the city of legendary traffic jams and every movement and trip around the city must be well timed, otherwise you'll find yourself in traffic for hours; It is called rush hour, yet nothing moves!" she added.

It was a medium-sized hotel with a friendly atmosphere. At the hotel's reception, the lady at the counter confirmed their booking and handed Petra the keys to their room.

"You're welcome. Please, relax and make yourselves at home here in our hotel," said the receptionist with a genial smile.

"Thank you," replied Petra.

The receptionist subsequently asked one of the chambermaids, Lucy, to show the guests their room.

"I hope you'll enjoy your stay here," said Lucy, after ushering the new arrivals to their room. "In our hotel, we take great pride in offering the best services in town," she added.

Later in the day, Jenny and her mother decided to take a stroll around the area near their hotel, hoping to get a feel for the neighbourhood.

The following morning, they hailed a taxi to head downtown and meet with Sandra, their tour guide, to plan their exploration of the city. Sandra suggested several must-see attractions, including a visit to Alagba, the famous giant male land tortoise believed to have resided in the palace of the ancient town of Ogbomoso for an astonishing 324 years.

"Wow, that's fascinating!" exclaimed Petra, intrigued by Sandra's suggestion.

"I'm also eager to explore the cultural artefacts in the museum and witness the traditional masquerades," added Jenny, perched on the edge of her seat with excitement.

"Absolutely. Those are already included in your itinerary," Sandra confirmed with a smile. "We have a rich cultural heritage to explore here."

The next morning, Jenny, and her mother, accompanied by Sandra, set out for the first leg of their city tour. They were greeted by bustling streets filled with noise and activity as they ventured out from their hotel.

Meanwhile, in her small room-office within the hotel, Lucy, the chambermaid, drifted off to sleep at her desk. Unbeknownst to her, she was also experiencing an out-of-body journey as her witchcraft body joined a coven session. The witches and wizards were gathered around a fire, singing and dancing, while an old man tended to a boiling pot. Lucy's trance was abruptly interrupted by Olademeji, her boss, entering the room.

"Lucy! What are you doing?" he demanded.

"Uh, good morning... I mean, good afternoon, Sir," Lucy stammered, attempting to regain her composure.

"You haven't answered my question. What are you doing?" Olademeji pressed.

"I was just... um, taking a quick nap," Lucy admitted, feeling flustered.

"Sleeping on the job? It's barely past eleven in the morning. This can't happen again," Olademeji warned sternly. "Understood?"

"Yes, sir! Yes, sir!" Lucy replied hastily.

The following day, a delegation of witches and wizards from neighbouring countries, along with a special visitor from Nogokpo village in Ghana, convened in Lagos. They were members of Weafric2w, a clandestine league with influence across sub-Saharan Africa and beyond. The elders of the group had gathered urgently to address the deteriorating health of their leader and explore potential remedies.

Upon their arrival, they were warmly greeted by Sabon-Gari, an enchanter and occult wizard, "For the bond!" they greeted one another warmly and thereafter proceeded to the residence of their leader. When the elders arrived, they were ushered into the house by Yemisi, Jaja's most senior wife, before promptly going in to see Jaja who was looking frail and lying motionless on his sickbed in one of the inner rooms of the spooky quiet interior, his condition grave and concerning to all.

Jaja, whom the witches and wizards called the GM, or Grand Master, was the unchallenged supreme leader of the Weafric2w; He had a huge incredibly dark background to his life and was widely feared because of his spiritual powers and nobody in the world of the witches and wizards in the continent could do anything without his permission. The leader was in a critical condition following the ravages of a strange illness and the very rare condition was one piece of a puzzle that had left him in a permanent vegetative state with progressive memory loss and without any prospects of improvement. And despite the miraculous advance of science in Nogokpo, the magic city where medical treatment had much improved, no physician in the land could find a cure for his life-threatening ailment. Nevertheless, the witches and wizards of Nogokpo were determined to do everything possible to save their leader and the sick leader had since clung on to life as if certain his much-needed help would come.

A few weeks earlier, Jaja was admitted to one of the big hospitals in Lagos where the ailment that had kept him bedridden for more than six months now was diagnosed as Viral Encephalitis and Neuro Degeneration, which the medical people interpreted as a loss of all functions. But, after some weeks in the hospital the doctors found he was emaciating and dying with his case becoming hopeless as the days went by, they recommended sending him overseas for medical attention.

As Jaja's health continued to decline, the elders of Weafric2w grew increasingly concerned. They reached a collective decision that conventional medical treatment at a hospital was not the solution for their leader. Instead, they opted to bring him back to his home, where they hoped alternative methods could revive him.

The house where Jaja resided was grand and spacious, reflecting his esteemed position within the community. As the elders navigated through the corridors, they passed through a lavishly decorated living room adorned with eccentric furniture and peculiar artefacts. Sofas formed a semicircle around a central table, creating an inviting space for gatherings. A portrait of Jaja in ceremonial attire adorned one wall, while a set of dining furniture occupied another side of the room. A substantial bookshelf dominated one corner, displaying a vast collection of literary works and mystical tomes.

Venturing further into the inner chambers, some of which lay shrouded in darkness, the elders encountered rooms filled with valuable ornaments and artefacts. However, the room where Jaja lay was a stark contrast to the opulence elsewhere in the house. Lightly furnished with understated decor, it exuded a sense of simplicity and solemnity. An original fireplace provided warmth, while exposed ark beams added a rustic charm to the ambience. Animal skins adorned the walls, alongside large portraits of Jaja, emphasizing his significance within the witchcraft community.

Rows of mirrors adorned one side of the room, serving as portals to the spiritual realm in the realm of witches and wizards. Among them was a coveted holographic magic mirror, hidden within Jaja's closet. Across from the mirrors stood a large black wardrobe, concealing mysteries and secrets within its depths. A full-length mirror positioned nearby had the unique ability to reflect a 360-degree image of anyone standing before it, a testament to Jaja's mastery of the arcane arts.

Near the doorway leading back to the living room sat an aquarium housing seven fishes. The significance of this specific number remained shrouded in mystery, known only to Jaja himself. In one of the more secluded chambers, Jaja kept a collection of enigmatic objects, invisible to the naked eye but possessing potent magical properties in the realm of witchcraft.

"Has he eaten anything?" asked Mthembu, who was momentarily playfully running one of his fingers through the glass of the aquarium and following the movement of one of the fishes inside that soon swarmed to the top and gulping as if ready to eat.

"No-o, my dear. I prepared him some food this morning, but he refused to even touch it," replied Yemisi.

"Haba, GM," said Mthembu, turning towards the sick leader on the bed, "please, why don't you eat something? Don't you know that food is the first and even the best medicine?" he implored the leader who did not move a finger.

After seeing the leader, the team emerged from the room leading to the inner chamber and headed straight to another larger room for their special meeting. Here in the conference room, three mirrors on star-shaped frames hung on the wall and a solitary lamp burned dimly on a table surrounded by outlandish-looking chairs.

Hardly had the wizards and the witches settled in the dimly lit room around the glow of the small flickering light when the image of a man appeared in the largest mirror that was hanging on the wall in the room. The image was that of Sanko, one of the elders from the neighbouring Benin Republic, who was joining his colleagues in the high-level discussion via video conferencing.

"For the bond," Sanko greeted the others as his image appeared in the mirror.

"For the bond," they replied.

"Mr. Sanko, you're coming late again and even joining us by video," said Kabila.

"Oh, don't blame him," cut in Toyosi, "You know, while we 're following the GMT, the one the white men call Greenwich Mean Time, his own time is the BMT or the Black Man's Time," he added jokingly.

"Please, leave Sanko alone, we're here for a more serious business!" said Sabon Gari. "Our GM's situation is a dilemma with no easy solution, and we need to begin right away!" He added.

Each of the participants had come to the conference with a part of the special ingredients needed to prepare the magic potion that was required to save their sick leader: "The hairs and claws of a male lion," said Kabila, placing the objects on the table with his left hand.

"The feathers of the Titibiti," said Toyosi, laying on the table the feathers of a very rare bird that was locally regarded as the king of birds.

Then, Babatunde, the herbalist, reached into his bag with his left hand and brought out some herbs, the roots of some rare plants and the bark of certain trees found in the deep forests. He set them down on the table.

"Here, I have the seashells and cowry shells from the south coast as well as some alligator pepper, bitter kola and other medicinal herbs," said Malaika, depositing the items on the table as well.

"And here are seven eggs of the cock in the evil forest and, here, wrapped inside these leaves, is the discarded scaly layers of a snake," said Sabon-Gari, carefully placing the wrapped leaves and the seven little eggs half the size of golf balls on the table in the same fashion.

"Here, in this container, I 've trapped a python's shadow, and in this other container, I've got the hairs and fingernails of a mermaid, which some of you here said would be hard to get.' said Sanko, purring with satisfaction from one of the mirrors on the wall.

Mthembu looked at Sanko in the mirror and smiled, he knew the latter was indirectly referring to him. Just then, Sanko emerged from the surface of the mirror, stepped on the floor, and carefully placed the two small, sealed boxes, the size of matchboxes, on the table before sitting down with his colleagues.

When they had finished, Mthembu, who was the highest-ranking wizard at the meeting cleared his throat and was about to speak when Caddy, the blind old witch and one of the confidants and special advisers of the sick leader, suddenly cried out cryptically, "Oyimbo! Oyimbo!

Ah, if you could see what I see!" All eyes suddenly turned towards the witch, whom some of the wizards at the meeting were curious to find out whether she would make good her promise of coming with the legs of a snake.

"Yes, all these ingredients we surely need to prepare the portion," began Caddy, "but, above all, we will need this oyimbo blonde girl to rejuvenate our GM. This girl, and not a snake's legs, is the indispensable element and the last piece of the jigsaw to save him." she declared.

"Oyimbo blonde girl?" asked Sanko in bewilderment, not sure what the blind witch was talking about - the others in the room were equally puzzled.

"Who is this oyimbo blonde girl?' asked Boniface, who had a little hump on his back.

Caddy, who had hitherto been surreptitiously sneaking a look into her divination calabash, then, carefully carried her crystal ball and placed it on the table in front of her colleagues.

"Oyimbo mwanamke kuonekana. Uchawi, Chabun-nagun-gamugg!" she muttered and waved her hand over the calabash.

Just then, the face of a young charming teenage fair-haired girl appeared on the face of the intangible screen of the calabash. It was the image of Jenny, the German teenager, who was on a visit with her mother to Nigeria.

"Behold! Behold!" cried Caddy. 'Search no further... the answer, the answer is here! This teenage girl is the last element we need to make the medicinal preparation complete!" exclaimed Caddy, and like someone in a trance stared blankly into the dark recesses of the room.

The other wizards peered curiously and marvelled at the image of the beautiful young girl with a luxurious mane in the divination calabash in front of them.

"But how and where can we find this girl?" queried Toyosi, known affectionately as Smally among his peers, who, despite being his late forties, maintained a youthful appearance that defied his true age. His diminutive stature and cherubic face masked a formidable presence within the world of witchcraft. Despite appearing shy and unassuming to the outside world, within the realm of magic, Smally commanded respect as a seasoned and ruthless wizard, his reputation built upon a history of dark deeds. Recognizing his prowess, he had been elevated to the esteemed position of an elder, a title typically reserved for accomplished witches and wizards of Weafric2w.

Caddy then divulged to her colleagues that the young woman they sought was within their territory. She proceeded to outline the details of how and where they could locate her. Following their discussion, Iyabor, accompanied by two other witches, was tasked with retrieving the blonde girl as foreseen by the oracle.

Despite the directive coming from higher authorities, Iyabor and her team adhered to protocol by following administrative procedure. They sought the approval of Sankara, the regional head from Dakar, who also served as the spiritual leader of the area encompassing the hotel in Lagos. before proceeding with their mission. Upon meeting with Sankara, Iyabor wasted no time in making the purpose of their mission known. The commandant subsequently appointed Fatoumata, one of his underlings, to lead the three to the hotel where the German girl was lodging.

Coincidentally, Petra found herself absent from the room on the fateful night when the witches and the wizard descended upon Jenny. Unbeknownst to her, she had made plans with Sandra two days before to enjoy some leisure time away from their accommodations. Anticipating an evening of relaxation and entertainment, they had eagerly scheduled their outing to coincide with a vibrant variety show and concert hosted at the hotel's bar.

Before departing for the event, Petra tenderly bade her daughter good night, bestowing a gentle kiss upon Jenny's forehead. Although initially invited to accompany them, Jenny had opted to stay behind, feeling weary from the day's earlier activities. Thus, with heartfelt well-wishes exchanged, Petra and Sandra embarked on their evening of revelry, leaving Jenny to rest peacefully in their absence.

On arrival at the hotel under the cover of darkness, Fatoumata put a mark on the doorframe of Jenny and Petra's room, and like thieves in the dark of night, the four went into the room as little rats, transforming once again into humans once they were inside.

The three witches carefully passed Jenny over to Fatoumata, who scrutinized her with a critical eye before relinquishing her back to the witches. With Jenny now in their possession, the witches were primed to execute their mission.

"I'm getting a particularly sweet vibe from this adorable little girl," whispered Itohan, one of the three witches. "Let me handle her," she offered eagerly.

But Iyabor, the team leader, swiftly intervened, lightly clapping Itohan on the wrist. "No, hands off!" she admonished. "This one is mine... and I'm doing her for the Grand Master!" The witches were convinced that whoever successfully retrieved this girl to aid their leader would be richly rewarded and possibly promoted.

Approaching Jenny lying on the bed, Iyabor hypnotized her before gently placing a mark on her forehead. This invisible mark signified that Jenny was now under their control, a possession of their coven. Through this mark, the witches and wizards could keep a watchful eye on her, establishing a spiritual connection with Jenny.

As Jenny drifted in and out of consciousness, she felt a surreal combination of dream and reality. Shadowy figures resembling animated drawings seemed to move about the room, their forms blurry and indistinct. Although she sensed something amiss, she found herself unable to articulate her distress, trapped in a semi-conscious state of helplessness.

Meanwhile, as the witches carried out their sinister deeds in the hotel, a Christian congregation convened an all-night vigil service in a nearby church. The preacher, fervently brandishing his Bible, addressed the congregation with urgency: "Many among us have long been ensnared by the dark forces of bewitchment," he declared. "The adversary prowls about like a roaring lion, seeking whom he may devour. Isaiah 59:7 warns us of their ceaseless plotting, their insatiable thirst for evil deeds, leaving devastation in their wake."

Urging the faithful to fortify themselves against these malevolent forces, the preacher invoked divine intervention. "We must render ourselves indigestible to the powers of darkness," he proclaimed. "Through the grace of God, we shall emerge victorious over oppression. Let us unite in prayer, invoking the name of Jesus to rebuke the forces of darkness and cleanse our souls from evil!"

Meanwhile, in Jenny's hotel room, the witches proceeded with the final step of their ritual to spiritually capture her. Suddenly, as if the universe itself intervened, an unseen surge of energy permeated the hotel, accompanied by a mysterious luminous glow that materialized within Jenny's room. The ethereal light, inexplicably appearing and vanishing in a mesmerizing dance, confounded the witches, its source eluding their comprehension. It flickered unpredictably, resembling a distant signal visible to the naked eye, evading their attempts to decipher its nature.

Unable to concentrate amidst the enigmatic spectacle, and wary of revealing their identities in the luminous glow, the witches reluctantly abandoned their mission, hastening their departure from the room. Simultaneously, Petra, sensing a foreboding unease in her spirit while attending the show, felt compelled to check on her daughter.

Awakening from her troubled slumber, Jenny found herself engulfed in a whirlwind of emotions. Unable to return to sleep, she grappled with the surreal events of the night, her consciousness inundated with vivid images and lingering sensations that defied the boundaries of dreams. The unsettling experience left her questioning reality and struggling to make sense of the inexplicable occurrences.

Did it happen, or did I just dream it?" she muttered to herself, bleary-eyed from lack of sleep; She was also feeling physically tired as though she did a tedious job during the night; She could not get the thought out of her head.

Just then, the door opened. It was Petra, who hurriedly walked in. She was surprised to see her daughter awake at the time. "Is everything alright?" she inquired. Jenny rushed into her mother's arms crying. "Mama, a strange thing happened to me while I was sleeping," said Jenny. She then went on to narrate her experience to her mother.

"You only had a nightmare," replied Petra. "Don't bother yourself about it because sometimes it happens," she told her daughter. However, the experience left a strong impression on Jenny that day and she couldn't think of anything else.

The next day, it was time for the tourists to leave. Altogether, they had a good time and an enjoyable tour. Petra had made few friends. In the morning, before their departure, Lucy, who had been especially nice came around and they engaged in a warm interactive session.

About two hours before their departure, Sandra arrived to pick up the tourists to the airport, and thereafter they took their flight back to Germany.

Meanwhile, the morning after their unsuccessful attempt to get Jenny in the hotel, the three witches were summoned to the coven where Iyabor narrated their experience to some of the elders. "We have never seen anything like that light, and we do not quite know what behaves like that; The mysterious light had us stumped and I don't think that was ordinary light," said Iyabor.

"Just listen to yourself!" cut in Sabon-Gari. "Witches who cannot fly! You have failed in your simple assignment, and I am highly disappointed in you!" He barked, gnashing his teeth.

"Master, have I ever embarked on a mission without completing it?" Asked Iyabor.

"You have always delivered in your various assignments, and we thought we could trust you with this very important one," answered Sabon-Gari, still seething with anger.

The three witches were in a quiet sombre mood, their faces edged with dismay as their leader berated and dressed them down. His reproach was a heavy knock and a wicked blow to their pride. They hung their heads in shame and stared blankly at the floor.

Later in the day, the elders of the Weafric2w met and decided to try again to get Jenny. To avoid another failure, Sabon-Gari volunteered to personally head the team. After sundown, Sabon-Gari decided to check up the fair-haired 'oyinbo' girl in his divination calabash. "She must be on our radar if that lazy Iyabor actually succeeded in putting the mark on her that would allow us to monitor her activities and communicate with her." he murmured to himself. "Oyinbo mwanamke ... Nionyeshe uso wako

... Uchawi ! Chaubun-nagun-gamugg!" the leader recited, after going through the opening ritual.

Suddenly, Jenny's image flickered to life on the screen of the enchanted calabash, surrounded by cowry shells that amplified its mystical power. However, the signals received by the Weafric2w radar's global positioning system indicated a perplexing discovery—Jenny was not within the vicinity of the hotel, but rather, her presence seemed to elude detection, evading the radar's reach.

"What? She's not in the hotel?" exclaimed the leader, his frustration evident in his voice. Despite the distance, the ability to summon Jenny's image into the calabash affirmed his continued influence over her. The wizard took solace in knowing that with the mark bestowed upon her, he retained the means to exert control over her, provided he maintained surveillance over her movements.

Determined to ascertain Jenny's whereabouts, the leader deactivated the calabash and retrieved his holographic mirror—a powerful tool equipped with advanced tracking capabilities. Adjusting the intricate knobs within the mirror's mechanisms, he meticulously calibrated its positioning and navigation systems to pinpoint Jenny's exact location in her newfound environment.

Opening the Tracker app embedded within the magical mirror, the leader initiated a search for the lost subject. With a series of taps, the mirror displayed the coordinates of Jenny's last known location, juxtaposed against her current whereabouts. Conjuring Jenny's image within the mirror's interface, he placed his thumb over the invisible mark on her forehead, zooming in to discern her precise orientation.

However, despite the mirror's revelation of Jenny's distant location, the leader's mental state hindered his immediate comprehension of the situation. It took a moment for him to fully grasp the implications of Jenny's remote presence, and when realization finally dawned upon him, he was overcome with a profound sense of dismay—Jenny was situated in a territory far removed from her previous physical presence, leaving the leader utterly devastated by the revelation.

"She's gone! She's gone!" he kept muttering to himself while shaking his head in disbelief.

This was a matter of great importance and he felt he must inform the others immediately about Jenny's departure. Slowly, Sabon-Gari packed up his divination paraphernalia and called Caddy, the blind old witch, on the telephone.

"The bird has flown!" said Sabon-Gari on the phone.

"Meaning what?" asked Caddy curiously.

"The oyimbo girl has left our principality! She's gone!" answered the rattled leader.

The news hit the old witch like a thunderbolt. "That girl cannot go anywhere!" Caddy exploded in a trembling voice. "Without the caterpillar, there can be no butterfly! Whether she's gone to the moon or back to her mother's womb, we must find her! There's no other way!" submitted Caddy with a note of definitiveness.

The witches and wizards were shattered by the news of Jenny's departure, and they were filled with an overwhelming sense of sadness; They believed the chance of saving their leader had now been thrown into great uncertainty.

Worried by the development and because it was a matter of extreme importance, some of the emergency committee elders of the Weafric2w converged on an Iroko tree that night for an extraordinary meeting to work out their next step.

"But we can get another Oyinbo girl." Mulumba proposed after they had all taken their seats.

"No! No substitute! This one is different!" retorted Caddy. "You cannot prepare an omelette without eggs and only that blonde oyimbo girl has the seal to save our GM! She's the vital element and a crucial part of the ingredients we need to revive him - Fate sent her to us, but we've lost her out of our carelessness!" she added, with a feeling of hopelessness. There was a deafening silence in the next few seconds with disappointment written on their faces.

"By the way, where is this oyinbo girl from?" asked Toyosi, finally breaking the silence.

"We heard she's from Germany." offered Babatunde.

"So, now, we will have to go to Germany to get her?' asked Boniface.

"Yes, ...yes, everything points to that possibility.' replied Sabon-Gari, almost before Boniface could finish his question. "What this means is that we will now require the collaboration of our best and brightest on an international level precisely to get the lady and bring her back to our land - The inability of those lazy three who could not carry out simple instruction has left us in this dilemma." He continued, with a grim sense of inevitability, while simultaneously picking up his hat that was resting on one of the tree branches.

"If I knew they'd mess up I'd have been there personally," said Kabila.

"Indeed, the work begins from here and we will embark on the important assignment, please, all of you should prepare," replied Mthembu.

"Let's meet again, today in the coven at the hour to discuss it and as a matter of urgency take a decision. For the bond!" Said Babatunde.

"Okay. then… for the bond!" Sabon-Gari, the ruthless operator greeted the others while simultaneously letting himself go by dropping off from the treetop before transforming into a bird in mid-air and flying off.

"For the bond!" the others replied while flying off on their magic palm fronts, while the others flew off as birds.

Chapter 3

Nogokpo

The village of Nogokpo, nestled in the heart of West Africa, seemed like any other rural community at first glance. However, behind its serene façade lay a deeper story and secrets that defy its outward appearance. Tucked away from mainstream civilization, Nogokpo is a refuge for those shunned by their own communities due to accusations of witchcraft or confessions thereof. Here, amidst the quaint simplicity of rural life, dwell individuals forced to forsake everything familiar—homes, families, and friendships—under the weight of societal stigma.

Yet, what sets Nogokpo apart is its dual nature, straddling both the physical and spiritual realms. By day, it resembles any other impoverished rural enclave, its landscape marred by poverty and neglect. But as the sun sets, the village undergoes a metamorphosis, revealing its hidden identity—the enigmatic Weafric City.

Nestled at the heart of a triangular expanse bordered by Tantuo to the north-west and Kokoligu in Northern Ghana, Weafric City emerges as a realm untouched by the mundane. Accessible only to witches and wizards through mystical portals, this ethereal metropolis stands in stark contrast to its earthly counterpart. Characterized by towering structures, immaculate streets, and meticulous organization, it exudes an otherworldly beauty that captivates the senses.

Despite its grandeur, Weafric City remains veiled from the prying eyes of ordinary mortals. Known only to the initiated members of the Weafric fraternity, it serves as the clandestine nerve centre of African witchcraft, where decisions of paramount importance are deliberated and executed. Through their collective knowledge and arcane abilities, the witches, and wizards of Nogokpo continue to shape and nurture this hidden sanctuary where top decisions are made, safeguarding its secrets from the outside world.

The city of Nogokpo stood as a bastion of advanced technology, its defences bolstered by innovations inspired by the humble spider. Utilizing the extraordinary properties of spider silk, Nogokpo's scientists engineered cutting-edge systems to safeguard their realm.

At the heart of Nogokpo's defences lay the Meter Wave sparse array synthetic impulse radar, a marvel of engineering that spanned the sky, tirelessly scanning for threats. Woven with strands of the finest spider silk, this radar system boasted unparalleled sensitivity and coverage, providing an impenetrable shield against intruders.

But the ingenuity of Nogokpo's scientists extended far beyond mere surveillance. Through exhaustive research, they unravelled the secrets of spider silk, unlocking its potential for myriad applications. Mimicking the spider's ability to spin fluid protein into resilient threads, they harnessed this remarkable material to create a variety of groundbreaking inventions.

From advanced software to cutting-edge hardware, every gadget in Nogokpo was seamlessly integrated with the city's sophisticated radar network. Anchored in Ni, Nogokpo's own Silicon Valley, these radar systems formed the backbone of the city's surveillance infrastructure. Empowered by advanced algorithms, they facilitated precise tracking of targets, whether distant or nearby, enabling the city to maintain a vigilant watch over its domain.

Thus, fuelled by the wonders of spider silk and guided by visionary innovation, Nogokpo stood as a testament to the boundless potential of human ingenuity.

As the witching hour approached, Festac Town in Lagos was cloaked in darkness, with only the faint glow of distant street lights piercing the night. Atop one of the houses, a mysterious owl settled onto the roof, its keen eyes scanning the surroundings with an air of anticipation. With each low hoot, the owl seemed to communicate with the shadows, its head swivelling to catch every sound.

Suddenly, a bat flitted into view, its erratic flight drawing the owl's attention. With remarkable agility, the owl tracked the bat's path, its cylindrical eyes fixed on the elusive prey. Despite the tempting opportunity for a midnight feast, the owl remained focused on its mission.

In a swift and silent descent, the owl glided toward a door, seamlessly slipping through the narrow gap beneath. Inside, Queen lay sound asleep, unaware of the mystical visitor about to enter her room. With a subtle transformation, the owl shed its feathery guise, revealing the form of a woman poised for her clandestine task.

The lady was Lucy who worked as a chambermaid in the hotel. She, like many of the other witches in Nogokpo, mostly preferred the owl bird form for delivering their messages and for carrying out some of their other nightly activities. Interestingly, unlike the Bats and other birds of prey that were also active during the dark hours, the owl, on the whole, benign and thought to be endowed with solemn wisdom, have to a large extent insinuated themselves into the peoples' affairs and their sober habits, choosing to live in derelict and desolate places, as well as their mostly nocturnal nature and predatory instinct and adaptation to night hunting make them attractive and stand them in good stead to the African witches and wizards.

Queen lay on her bed, seemingly asleep, but within her, something extraordinary was happening. Her consciousness began to separate from her physical form, initiating an otherworldly journey into the realm of the unseen. This out-of-body experience wasn't a dream; it was a vivid and unsettling experience that defied explanation.

As her ethereal witchcraft body floated above her sleeping body, Queen felt a profound sense of detachment. She reached out tentatively, touching her spectral form to confirm its reality. Astonishment washed over her as she realized she was simultaneously the observer and the observed, existing in two states at once.

Amidst her bewilderment, distant sounds drifted into her awareness – the rhythmic beat of drums, the haunting melody of distant chanting. The vibrations pulsed through her, drawing her towards their source with an irresistible force. Her senses, sharpened by the uncanny experience, absorbed every nuance of the auditory tapestry surrounding her.

A soft chuckle shattered the stillness, and Queen turned to find Lucy, her friend and unwitting guide, standing beside her. There was a knowing gleam in Lucy's eyes, a silent acknowledgement of their shared journey into the mystic. It was Lucy who had introduced Queen to the world of witchcraft, subtly weaving her into its intricate web.

Recalling the innocuous snack shared earlier, Queen realized the true nature of Lucy's gift – a potion hidden within the food, now stirring the dormant energies within her. With a silent invitation, Lucy beckoned Queen to join her, to embrace the mysteries awaiting them in the coven's embrace.

"You're now one of us!" said Lucy, with a sly look on her face.

"Me? One of you?" asked Queen, rather surprised.

"Yes, you're now a witch!" replied Lucy. And, then she added, "You're now one of us. I'm here to pick you up with me to the coven."

"To the coven? But I ...," said Queen.

"Queen, we need to be on our way! We don't have much time. I will explain everything to you later," cut in Lucy. As she was saying this, she took her friend by the hand and led her out through the door that was closed.

Together, Lucy and Queen embarked on a surreal journey, traversing the ethereal plane on a palm front guided by Lucy's adept navigation. As they approached the coven's gathering place, they were greeted by ushers who doubled as cup bearers, their senses finely attuned to the subtlest signs of the arcane.

Entering the coven, they were enveloped by an atmosphere thick with the energy of dark magic. Members, old and new, gathered for the evening's proceedings, each eager to share their malevolent exploits. It was a time for confessions, a twisted form of camaraderie among practitioners of the forbidden arts.

Fatoumata, her face twisted with satisfaction, revealed her latest act of cruelty – the malicious manipulation of her husband's second wife, Amina, rendering her barren and desperate for solace. Lucy, in hushed tones, explained the insidious nature of Fatoumata's curse to Queen, highlighting the devastating consequences lurking beneath its surface.

Cecilia's confession followed, detailing her vindictive retribution upon her ex-lover's career, leaving him powerless and impotent in the face of his ambitions. Lucy, ever the informant, whispered to Queen about the sinister spell of motion without movement, or MWM, its insidious effects rendering its victims powerless despite their efforts.

As the macabre revelations continued, Dora's admission shocked even the most callous among them. With chilling nonchalance, she confessed to the ultimate act of betrayal, "I have finally killed my mother!" She announced. In the twisted hierarchy of their cult, such a heinous act was rewarded with unparalleled prestige, the blood of kin, or first blood, offering a dark path to ascension.

Amidst the darkness, Lucy whispered to Queen of Cecilia's formidable influence and Dora's grim ascension, revealing the true depths of their power. In this world of shadows and secrets, alliances were forged in blood and power was measured in the darkness of the soul.

After Dora's heinous act in the spirit realm resulted in the death of her mother, her physical demise unfolded just as meticulously planned. Two days later, a tragic accident on the road claimed her life, along with several other unsuspecting passengers. It was a chilling manifestation of her dark intentions, orchestrated with precision from the depths of the coven.

As Dora proudly recounted her deeds to her fellow witches, the room erupted in applause, a twisted celebration of her malevolence. Their approval was palpable, their faces contorted with gleeful satisfaction. Lucy, with a sinister smile, exchanged a glance with Queen, who sat in stunned disbelief, grappling with the horror of their confessions.

For the Weafric witches and wizards, revelling in tales of bloodshed and misery was second nature. Their existence thrived on the suffering of others, and the anguish of their victims was their perverse delight. Queen, however, felt a profound sense of anguish at the depravity of their deeds.

In a hushed whisper, Queen turned to Lucy, her voice laced with incredulity. "But why?" she asked, her mind reeling from the sheer brutality of Dora's actions. "How could she commit such unspeakable acts?"

Lucy's response was sharp, her tone unapologetic. "They had to die," she declared. "Not every accident is as it seems. Innocent lives are often sacrificed for our purposes."

As the session ended, the initiation of new members commenced, marking their induction into the dark fraternity. Led by Boniface, the newcomers were ushered into the inner sanctum, where they partook of a mysterious black liquid, a symbol of their transformation. In this sacred space, they were imbued with the power to shape-shift into their chosen animals or objects, a pivotal step in their journey into the world of witchcraft.

With the presentation of their magical brooms, the initiates were initiated into their newfound independence, forever bound by the dark waters of the coven. As the saying went in the realm of Weafric2w, the waters of initiation forever altered the course of a witch's destiny, marking the beginning of their true identity.

At the end of the meeting, Lucy and Queen went outside. "There are certain things I feel you should know and as a friend, I'm going to show you great and marvellous things," said Lucy. "First, I've a surprise for you; I'm taking you on a visit to Nogokpo," she went on.

"A visit to Nogokpo?" asked Queen, with a quizzical expression on her face. Queen had heard much about Nogokpo, the quiet and obscure little village where social outcasts were confined and a place where life seemed to have stood still. So, she wondered what they would be doing visiting such as place.

"I know what you're thinking, but I want to let you know that for a glimpse into Africa's possible future, look no further than Nogokpo, which is a world within a world, and I can assure you that some of the things you'll find there will blow your mind." said Lucy, pausing with a smile playing between her lips to let her friend reflect on what she was telling her.

Then looking away from Queen and into the bushes and then further into the big dark night, Lucy chuckled as her eyes drifted towards the sky and then at the moon that seemed to be peeping from behind the blanket of the leaves of the tree beside her.

The two flew on Lucy's broom to the village of Nogokpo. When they arrived, Lucy decided they walked the distance through the lush jungle of the unexplored region to the heart of the jungle where the water body that was the portal to the world of the Weafric2w lay.

"In our world," Said Lucy, "the night is everything. To many, the night is terrifying, but the night is full of life. Stars cannot shine without darkness; we are the stars." Then, she paused and gently took Queen's hand as they walked down the gentle slope leading through the short and winding bush paths on their way to the spirit world of Nogokpo deep inside the luxuriant but mysterious rain forest. Normally, Lucy used to fly on her palm front to the City of Nogokpo, but this time, she decided to walk, so she could have some time to let her friend into some of their secrets.

"I want you to understand that our world today is governed by the spiritual realm," Lucy began, her voice carrying a weight of solemnity. "The unseen controls the seen. Everything we perceive in the physical world is orchestrated by forces beyond our sight. Most tangible objects are born from the intangible blueprints conceived in the minds of their creators. Before anything materializes in our reality, it takes form first in the spiritual domain," she explained, her words laden with mystery.

"I'm not sure I follow," Queen admitted, her brow furrowing with confusion.

"It's a profound concept," Lucy acknowledged. "Our realm of witchcraft operates with meticulous organization. To access Nogokpo, I'm not referring to the village you're familiar with, but rather the hidden enclave known as Weafric City, one must have a specific purpose. Nogokpo is a city of intricate design and structure, comprising twenty-five departments and faculties. Each department is governed by a leader and their assistants. There are departments dedicated to various aspects of life, such as religion, science, technology, and even fashion. For example, within the fashion department, there are subdivisions like cosmetics, encompassing creams, perfumes, and the like," Lucy elaborated, revealing a glimpse into the enigmatic city's inner workings.

As they traversed a winding path leading to a tranquil stream, Queen paused to pluck a leaf from a nearby tree. Continuing their journey, they descended a series of zigzagging trails until they reached a dense thicket. "In our world, where there exists a governing body in the physical realm, a corresponding authority exists in our realm," Lucy continued, her voice carrying a tone of authority. "There are leaders who oversee each territory. Even if I were to target you in this very street, I would need to adhere to protocol by seeking approval from the area's leader. They don't wield power over you directly," she divulged, shedding light on the hierarchy of their realm.

At that moment, the pair emerged from the thicket, revealing a secluded pond nestled amidst the foliage. Known as Lumbubashi, the mystical pond remained perpetually filled, unaffected by the scorching sun or the footprints of those who approached it. Legends spoke of its role as a gateway to the clandestine world of Weafric witches and wizards, its access guarded by invisible sentinels.

"Here, we are to obtain our boarding pass!" said Lucy jokingly, taking her partner's hand and stepping into the placid waters. Just then, the calm waters of the pond began to bubble and simmer.

"Open up to Lucy... open up, open up ...opa!" Lucy uttered the identification code.

The waters suddenly calmed after a few seconds, having recognized the visitor. "Look in the water," said Lucy to her friend. They both looked down and their faces were biometrically scanned from the images that appeared in the waters.

Just then, a sudden gentle breeze that was slowly rocking the leaves of the surrounding trees started sweeping in and as they looked, they could feel the gentle spiralling movement of their surroundings; Everything around them appeared to be moving around as though in a whirlpool washing machine. Queen held on to Lucy's hand tightly and closed her eyes frightened she was going to die.

As they ventured further into the pond, Queen noticed a faint haze enveloping them, stirring a sense of unease within her. Beyond the pond's edge, the landscape seemed to ripple and shift, as if transitioning to a different realm, its ambience subtly altering with each passing moment. It was an optical illusion, akin to witnessing the shifting of time zones.

Gradually, the disconcerting haze dissipated, revealing a breathtaking sight before them. Lucy, leading the way, guided Queen out of the water and through the overhanging branches, unveiling the hidden splendour of Nogokpo. Before them sprawled the majestic city in all its glory, a mesmerizing fusion of myth and mystery brought to life. Queen stood in awe, captivated by the newfound vista that unfolded before her eyes.

Taking a few steps closer, Queen marvelled at the skyline that stretched across the horizon. The towering futuristic skyscrapers, with their sleek, modern design, resembled structures from a utopian metropolis or a scene from a science fiction film. It was a revelation of a world she had never imagined existed.

From their vantage point, Queen and Lucy observed the bustling streets below, teeming with life. People navigated the thoroughfares on a variety of unconventional vehicles, ranging from woven baskets to lightweight rafts and even transparent inflatable balloons. It was a surreal sight, unlike anything Queen had ever witnessed, evoking a sense of wonder and curiosity.

As they descended from the hill and ventured onto the adjacent street, Queen couldn't shake the feeling of being watched. A bald vulture perched nearby, its keen gaze fixed upon them, while two other black birds hovered overhead before alighting on a nearby tree. These avian sentinels, known as watch-birds, played a crucial role in the city's surveillance, their vigilant eyes and keen instincts ensuring the safety and secrecy of Nogokpo. As Queen and Lucy passed by, the birds seamlessly transformed into covert spy cameras, their vigilant surveillance continuing unabated.

As Lucy and Queen strolled onward, they soon found themselves on a boulevard adorned with elegant fountains. The serene atmosphere of the place enveloped them, casting a spell of tranquillity over the first-time visitor. Queen couldn't help but be entranced by the serene yet futuristic ambience of the captivating city.

"Oh, my goodness, I've heard so much about this place in our folklore, but I never imagined it could be real!" Queen exclaimed, her eyes wide with wonder. "It's like stepping into a scene from a science fiction novel. This is Nogokpo?" she asked, her voice tinged with amazement.

"Yes, indeed, my dear. You've entered Nogokpo, but on a different plane of existence. It's a transformed world, a parallel community that many of us witches in Africa love to visit," Lucy explained, her tone tinged with pride. "The creators of Nogokpo had a vision for the future."

Lucy went on to describe the architectural marvels of Nogokpo, painting a picture of luxury and sophistication. The high-rise towers offered opulent residences complete with spas, pools, gyms, and meeting rooms, alongside an array of shops, restaurants, and hotels boasting round-the-clock concierge services. It was a place where luxury and modernity intertwined seamlessly—a sight to behold and an experience to savour.

Queen nodded in agreement; her senses fully engaged by the spectacle before her. Gone was the sleepy rural setting of Nogokpo; in its place stood a vibrant cityscape, teeming with life and pulsating with energy. Magnificent buildings rose majestically against the backdrop of a stunning environment, while the streets bustled with activity, inhabited by a diverse and dynamic populace.

"I have an old friend, Winnie, who lives not far from the city centre," Lucy remarked, a smile playing on her lips. "If you're up for it, we could pay her a visit."

"Okay, why not?" replied Queen. "So, it's true!" muttered Queen, after the two had walked for a while.

"What's true?" asked Lucy.

"So, these are the fabled and often talked about but rarely seen witches and wizards who are said to fly on brooms," said Queen.

On hearing that, Lucy smiled, her teeth gleaming white against the dark complexion of her face.

"Now, my friend, you truly have eyes!" replied Lucy.

"I wonder how the people in Lagos or Accra would feel when they see a witch flying on a palm front in the open?" said the new entrant.

A surprising response resonated from one of the small rocks scattered along the sidewalk, its mouth and teeth chattering as if alive. "They'll be surprised! They'll be surprised!" echoed the rock, its tone oddly melodious.

Another rock nearby, also sporting a mouth and teeth, chimed in with a squeaky female voice. "Oh, yes! They'll surely be intrigued by the witch. People here hold anything that flies in high esteem," it exclaimed, prompting a chorus of laughter from the surrounding rocks.

Lucy interjected, gesturing to the rocks dismissively. "Pay them no attention," she advised, before trailing off abruptly. Her gaze fixed on the faint impressions of human footprints in the sand behind them. Though the footprints were visible, the figure that had left them remained invisible, indicating a silent observer trailing them. Lucy sensed they were being monitored, likely by security personnel keeping an eye on the newcomer. "These are the gatekeepers," she whispered to her companion.

"Opa! Opa!" Lucy greeted the unseen watchers, motioning for Queen to do the same. "Opaopa," Queen echoed, just as the footprints abruptly changed direction in the sand and retreated.

As they continued toward the city centre, an elegantly attired elderly woman descended from the sky, gracefully landing before them. She rode atop a sleek glass vessel resembling an enclosed saucer, a symbol of her status and affluence in the city. Madam Jojo, the wife of a prominent city administrator, exuded authority, and sophistication. Beside her, her young maid soared gracefully on a palm frond, a stark contrast to her mistress's regal demeanour.

"Helloo, my Lucy! How are you doing today?" said Madam Jojo, with a wide grin.

"Ah, Madam Jojo. Nice to see you," replied Lucy.

"I haven't seen you around for quite a while, I hope you're keeping well?" asked the madam.

"Oh, I'm doing fine, thank you," answered Lucy.

"It's nice to see a new face here," said Madam Jojo, smiling at Queen.

"Oh, she's my friend, her name's Queen. She's a new entrant and a first-time visitor to our city," said Lucy.

"Hello, my dear," said Madam Jojo.

"Good day, madam," replied Queen.

"I'm just showing Queen around and hope to break her in as time goes on," said Lucy.

"That's alright, please do that, my Lucy." said Madam Jojo, and then she turned towards Queen, "You're welcome to our civilization, my dear! I hope Lucy's looking after you nicely?" she asked.

'Oh yes, she is! Thank you, madam!' replied Queen.

"Have a nice time with your friend and see you again, soon, Lucy." said the Madam and then flew off with her maid.

"She looks gorgeous," said Queen.

'Madam Jojo is a very influential woman in this city, and she belongs to the charmed circle,' Lucy remarked.

In the distance, Queen's gaze fell upon a majestic structure nestled on a steep hillside, catching the sunlight with a dazzling display of crystals and stalactites adorning its walls. It stood as a testament to Nogokpo's architectural brilliance, a sight to behold amidst the verdant landscape. Beside it, a smaller building adorned with ivy exuded charm, its facade a canvas for a vibrant floral arrangement that attracted butterflies flitting from bloom to bloom.

"That's the City Hall," Lucy explained, gesturing towards the imposing edifice.

"And just to the right, you'll see the taxi ranch with its fleet of driverless vehicles hovering in the air. On the other side, unconventional modes of transportation like the phantom cars cater to those seeking independent travel around the city. They serve both public and private needs, offering short hops or grand tours," she elaborated as Queen marvelled at the scene.

Before Lucy could finish, a horse-drawn carriage soared overhead, landing gracefully before City Hall. A man disembarked, accompanied by a woman and two feline companions. Suddenly, a retinue of albino attendants materialized, forming a protective circle around the man as they hovered on specially crafted palm fronds with spinning umbrella shades.

"Who's that?" Queen inquired, pointing to the horseman.

"That's Butaflica, one of the city's esteemed administrators," Lucy replied.

"And those albino guards are his retinue. He holds considerable sway in our governance," she added.

Observing Butaflica's departure, Queen's attention was drawn to a gleaming white tower nearby, crowned by a towering statue of Julius Mo, Nogokpo's revered founder. Nearby, a group of albino figures engaged in an enigmatic ritual, communicating in hushed tones without moving their lips.

"Those are the shadowy agents of our grand master, or S.A.G.M." Lucy explained, nodding towards the mysterious figures. "They undertake special tasks and safeguard our city under the leadership of Bunju, a master of esoteric knowledge," she disclosed, cautioning Queen against pointing at them.

As they continued their stroll, they approached a gravity-defying bridge resembling a serpent suspended in mid-air. Its sinuous form captivated onlookers, a testament to Nogokpo's blend of artistry and engineering prowess, drawing tourists from far and wide to marvel at its splendour.

"They say you cannot place something on nothing and expect it to stand, but not in Nogokpo. My sister, check out the Bengazoli bridge, a structural masterpiece that was constructed by one of the great wizards from North Africa." said Lucy. The bridge suddenly disappeared as they stepped into one of the conveyor tubes just below the bridge and the narrow tube suddenly began to expand like a balloon to accommodate the two and then slowly levitated with its occupants towards the bridge that now reappeared, before finally resting at the mouth of the high bridge that was shaped like the open mouth of a giant snake and the two stepped out unto the platform of the bridge.

From their vantage point, Queen marvelled at the breathtaking view of Nogokpo spread out before her, her eyes tracing the clusters of buildings in the distance as Lucy handed her a pair of gently rocking binoculars. Adjusting the lenses, she focused on the area Lucy pointed out.

"That's Ni," Lucy explained, gesturing towards the bustling hub on the horizon. "It's like the Silicon Valley of Nogokpo, the epicentre of technological innovation and research." Queen nodded, taking in Lucy's words as she adjusted the binoculars for a clearer view.

"In Ni, you'll find the heartbeat of our technological revolution," Lucy continued. "It's where all the major tech companies are based, and it serves as the nerve centre for monitoring and analysing everything happening in the city in real-time."

Lucy paused, allowing Queen to absorb the significance of Ni's role in Nogokpo's technological landscape.

"Here in Nogokpo, we believe that anything technology can achieve, witchcraft can replicate," Lucy explained. "Our scientists in Ni are constantly pushing the boundaries of discovery, engaging in fierce competition to stay ahead of the curve."

At the mention of Ni's secret projects, Queen's curiosity piqued even further.

"Ni houses some of the most advanced research facilities and laboratories, where scientists work on top-secret projects like artificial intelligence," Lucy revealed. "These endeavours are shrouded in secrecy, hidden from public knowledge, but they're at the forefront of technological advancement." She added.

Queen marvelled at the thought of the cutting-edge research and development happening within Ni's confines, realizing the depth of Nogokpo's technological prowess.

"Wao, that's unbelievable!" enthused Queen.

"Indeed, it is!" replied Lucy. "Remember, before we set out today, I told you that for a glimpse into Africa's possible future, you should look no further than Nogokpo. When I said that, I had the mini-Province of No in mind." She added, then waited for her companion to take it all in before continuing scholarly,

"And before I forget, it might also interest you to know that the new quantum leap in technological sophistication here in Nogokpo took off following the advancement of science beyond material unlike what they have in the West. First, I'd like to let you know that even though there's witchcraft and there's science, but, here in Nogokpo, science and witchcraft go hand in hand and following the emergence of Wi-sci, or the coming together of science and witchcraft to be precise, our superb scientists and engineers, inspired by progress and driven by the desire for adventure, are no longer bound by many of the technological constraints faced by their counterparts in the Western world and have as a result become more innovative.

Queen stood in awe, her mind reeling from the sheer magnitude of what she was witnessing. The breathtaking scenery stretched out before her, a testament to the wondrous world of Nogokpo. Lost in the spectacle, she took hesitant steps forward, absorbing every detail.

Suddenly, her reverie was interrupted by a peculiar sight. An elderly woman, carrying a basket brimming with a strange liquid, flew past her on a makeshift raft of light wood. Queen's eyes widened in surprise as she watched the woman navigate the air, seemingly defying gravity.

As the woman passed by, Queen noticed something peculiar about the basket. Despite its numerous open holes, the liquid inside remained mysteriously contained. It was as if some unseen force was at work, preventing the liquid from spilling out. Intrigued and bewildered by the encounter, Queen couldn't help but marvel at the strange sight.

"Watch where you are going, lady!" she shouted at Queen in a high-pitched voice fit for the opera.

"Oh, I'm sorry!" replied Queen.

"Next time, I 'm going to shock you by taking you on a visit to Boaboa, one of our late leader's beautiful orchards which lies about two miles south of Ni, to see the money trees." said Lucy.

"Huh... money trees?" asked Queen.

"Yes, the money trees," answered Lucy. "Ever seen money growing on trees?" she asked.

"Never... but I 've often heard people say that money doesn't grow on trees." answered the first-time visitor.

"Well, that phrase doesn't hold water here in Nogokpo and whoever came out with that coinage is either hopelessly unambitious or tragically uninformed, because there at Boaboa, the foreign currencies of some major Western countries do grow on some special trees in the same way fruits do, and when the notes that form the leaves of these special trees mature and are fully ripe, they're no different from the Western countries' actual banknotes.'" revealed Lucy.

"Wao, that sounds incredible!" said Queen.

"Indeed, it is!" replied Lucy. "Once upon a time, Helenia, the genius and legendary witch from Lampedussa visited Nogokpo and, to serve as a memorial of her visit and as a token of her love for Nogokpo, she decided to plant the special trees to show her host that money could grow on trees." she continued. "However, the arrangement was that everyone could only look but strictly forbidden, and I 'll repeat that, strictly forbidden to touch, pluck or use the foreign currencies," added Lucy.

"That sounds amazing. I'd like to see the trees now!" said Queen, like an excited kid anxiously waiting for a present.

"Don't worry, my darling, just relax." Replied Lucy. "On our next visit, I 'll take you to the field that has trees whose leaves bear different foreign currencies, with each tree producing specific notes of a particular country," Lucy promised.

The journey through Nogokpo's enchanting streets was like a voyage through a realm where nature and modernity danced in harmony. With Lucy as her guide, Queen revelled in every moment, pausing at every corner to soak in the sights and sounds of this magical city. The junction where seven roads converged was a bustling crossroads of energy and life, pulsating with the vibrant rhythm of the city.

As they strolled towards the city centre, Queen's senses were overwhelmed by the sheer splendour of Nogokpo. Towering skyscrapers reached towards the sky, their sleek designs a testament to the city's architectural prowess. Alongside, cascading waterfalls cascaded down rocky cliffs, while sparkling beaches beckoned with their azure waters.

The contrast between the opulence of Nogokpo and the poverty of neighbouring cities was stark, yet somehow, in this realm, it all seemed to coexist in perfect balance. Queen marvelled at the advancements of the Weafric witches and wizards, whose mastery over architecture and design was evident in every corner of the city.

Eventually, they reached Winnie's apartment, nestled in the southeastern quadrant of the city. As they settled in, a peculiar sight caught Queen's eye. A bunch of bananas sitting on a rack suddenly began to ring, vibrating with the urgency of an incoming call.

Winnie, unfazed by the unusual interruption, calmly approached the bananas and plucked one from the bunch. With a swift motion, she peeled back a portion of the skin, revealing a flash of light emanating from her hand. In an instant, the banana transformed into a sleek smartphone, its appearance unchanged from its fruity disguise. The voice at the other end was that of her boyfriend, James. He spoke excitedly, his voice crackling through the magical device he had fashioned from a mango, known as the

Mango-phone. James was inviting Winnie to a lavish party scheduled for the upcoming weekend, promising a night of revelry and entertainment in the heart of the city.

Queen watched in astonishment as Winnie effortlessly wielded her magical powers, seamlessly blending the mundane with the extraordinary. Queen's eyes widened. She had never seen a thing like that. She shot a sideways glance at Lucy.

"That's the "Bana-phone, one of the top-of-the-ranges mobile phones." Whispered Lucy.

While Winnie conversed with James, Queen's was captivated by an advertisement playing on the circular glass tube television set nearby. The device emitted a soft glow, its surface adorned with swirling lights that danced in hypnotic patterns. Queen was mesmerized as she watched a three-dimensional image of a lady promoting the latest innovation from one of Nogokpo's top electronic firms – the Paw-phone. The holographic display technology was a marvel, showcasing the city's cutting-edge advancements in communication.

In Nogokpo, competition among smartphone manufacturers was fierce, each vying to outdo the other with innovative features and captivating advertisements. Some stores even employed cameras equipped with advanced emotion recognition software, tailoring advertisements to match the mood of passersby. Meanwhile, massive billboards on the streets offered interactive experiences, seamlessly integrating with smartphones to engage users in new and immersive ways.

As Queen watched the advertisement, she was startled when the holographic presenter addressed her directly, referring to her as "gorgeous." The presenter then turned her attention to Lucy, inviting both her and Queen to experience the Paw-phone's unique features. With a wave of her hand, the holographic image demonstrated the phone's capabilities, showcasing its ability to control home appliances remotely.

With a flick of her finger, the presenter sliced a piece of pawpaw, magically transforming it into a slim smartphone. Demonstrating its functionality, she dialled a number on the transparent smartphone displayed on the table, showcasing its seamless integration with other devices. As the demonstration concluded, the holographic image receded into the television set, leaving behind a resounding endorsement of the Paw-phone: "P-phone, all you can ever dream of!"

"This company is one of the best examples of how forward-thinking visionaries here are using technology via smartphones in a practical way," said Lucy.

Queen was left mesmerized by the unusual show she'd just watched on the equally strange-looking television set. "The witches and wizards here seemed to be advanced in holographic technology, something I read about in science fiction novels and something that was still developing in the advanced world." cut in Queen before Lucy could finish.

"Oh, yes," replied Lucy. "By coupling the science of television with the science of laser beams, we can use a laser beam to create a 3-Dimensional image of anybody you want to talk to sitting right in this room so that the same conference is taking place in different places simultaneously. For instance, you can contact your friends in South Africa or Canada, and you can assemble them in laser beam images by dialling and asking each one to come on for a conversation," she added.

"Ah, so, Winnie, you bought it already and you didn't tell me!" exclaimed Lucy, simultaneously picking up a small container from the table.

"My, dear, what have I bought again and didn't tell you?' asked Winnie walking towards her guests. "Oh, you mean the... Sexometer?" she asked, while simultaneously giggling.

"Oh, yes, I bought it just yesterday but they're still very expensive at the moment," said Winnie, "I can't afford to take a risk with my guy and lose him to those hot sexy things in mini-skirts, and you know our guys' trousers nowadays don't rest on their waist. So, I told James to prove his love to me and convince me he wasn't flirting around with other chics and he suggested we go for the Sexometer." Winnie, who over the years had seen no end to the development of gadgets in Nogokpo, told her guests.

"Wao, I first saw the ad last week, soon, I intend to get one, too! So, how do you use it?" asked Lucy excitedly.

"The maker has different types of this product," replied Winnie. There's the one you insert in, down there and this is the one that mimics how protein folds into 3-Dimensional shapes. Once inserted, a version can fold itself into invisibility, while another type remains folded physically inside of you. But this one you're holding in your hands is my favourite and it's the injectable chip that could also be inserted under the skin in any part of the body.

Queen marvelled at the cutting-edge holographic technology showcased on the peculiar television set, feeling as though she had stepped into the pages of a science fiction novel. Before Lucy could elaborate further, Queen interjected with her observations, expressing awe at the advanced level of innovation among the witches and wizards.

Lucy nodded in agreement, explaining the intricacies of the holographic system. By harnessing the principles of television and laser beam technology, users could project lifelike 3D images of individuals into any space, enabling virtual gatherings and conferences across vast distances. Lucy painted a picture of the seamless connectivity offered by this technology, allowing users to interact with friends and loved ones from different parts of the world as if they were all present in the same room.

As the conversation unfolded, Winnie approached her guests, holding a small container in her hands. Lucy's eyes lit up with curiosity as she inquired about Winnie's recent purchase.

"Ah, so, Winnie, you bought it already and you didn't tell me!" exclaimed Lucy, simultaneously picking up a small container from the table.

"My, dear, what have I bought again and didn't tell you?' asked Winnie walking towards her guests. "Oh, you mean ...?" she asked, "Oh, yes, I bought it just yesterday but they're still very expensive at the moment," said Winnie, "I can't afford to take a risk with my guy and lose him to those hot sexy things in mini-skirts, and you know our guys' trousers nowadays don't rest on their waist. So, I told James to prove his love to me and convince me he wasn't flirting around with other chics and he suggested we go for the Sexometer." Winnie, who over the years had seen no end to the development of gadgets in Nogokpo, told her guests.

"Wao, I first saw the ad last week; Soon, I intend to get one, too! So, how do you use it?" asked Lucy excitedly.

With a playful giggle, Winnie revealed the intriguing device – the Sexometer – designed to monitor and analyse intimate interactions between partners, as they can gather all relevant biometric data about your sex life." Winnie elaborated on the various models available, describing how each version served a unique purpose. From discreet inserts to injectable chips, the Sexometer offered a range of options for users to monitor and enhance their intimate experiences. "With this latest magical invention, the days of having secret affairs and cheating by couples are over because the Sexometer will expose them all!" Exclaimed Winnie, as shared her plans to integrate the device into her relationship, her guests listened intently, intrigued by the possibilities offered by Nogokpo's latest technological marvels.

"Yes-o, there's nowhere to hide anymore for those playboys and playgirls out there!" added Lucy.

Soon, they had to leave and the two were back on the streets and on their way home. "Next time, I'll show you some of our other secrets here in Nogokpo; For instance, the finger recognition gadgets, mind you, not fingerprinting, but finger recognition as well as other wireless technologies that have been with us here for many years before coming to the West," said Lucy to her friend. "But, you know, there are other top-secret technologies here, many of which you won't find in the advanced world, which I cannot show you right now," she revealed.

However, something struck Queen as unusual. "But I can't understand...I can't understand why we have all these wonderful things here in the city and not introduce them to develop our region?" asked Queen, speaking more to herself than asking her companion the question.

"Sshhh, ssh!" Lucy cautioned her friend while simultaneously looking around and over her shoulder. "Perish the thought!" said Lucy. "Please, don't even think about it or let anyone hear that here. You know, that's precisely the problem. Our leaders in this city are averse to the idea of introducing our technologies and advanced discoveries here to the physical world of our region like they do in the West; They are satisfied with the status quo as they have all the necessary powers in this realm." she disclosed. "And, indeed, things are not difficult for us here, because if I want to travel, I don't use a car that pollutes the air, and I don't care for one. You can see how people get around here, it's easier.

"If our grand master, for instance, wanted to travel for a meeting say, in Sierra Leone or Morocco, he would sit down on his black chair in his room and fix his eyes on his mirror. His destination would appear in the mirror, and he'd project himself to that place in the presence of his host and in seconds he would be there," added Lucy.

"So, you mean, just like video conferencing?" asked Queen.

"Uhmm... yes, but it is better than what they call video conferencing today," replied Lucy revealingly.

Lucy mounted her broom and gestured to her companion to join her.

"Or would you like to disvirgin your broom and ride it home?" She asked.

"Oh yes, let's do it!" answered Queen as she mounted her broom.

The hyper-vivid, out-of-body visit to the advanced world of the Weafric witches and wizards had been a mind-blowing experience for her. And it was a very exciting trip flying for the first time on a broom.

"This city is sheer magic, and life here is so perfect and it's like catching a glimpse of the future!" admitted the enthralled first-time visitor. "Yes, in Nogokpo, reality has caught up with virtual reality and the city is perpetually being crafted with an eye on the future and that is why this place is a haven and the favourite haunt for us and a sanctuary from the outside world; It's a place of deep mystery and enchantment," replied Lucy, and then quickly added, "but much of our world is covered in secrecy and is well protected."

Chapter 4

The Send-Off Party

The long-awaited day had finally dawned – the extraordinary gathering of the Weafric witches and wizards was upon them. It was a historic occasion, the likes of which had never been seen before. The coven buzzed with anticipation as members from far and wide converged, dressed in their vibrant regalia, each outfit a testament to their unique magical prowess.

The purpose of the meeting was clear: to elect an acting leader and assemble a team tasked with a vital mission – to journey to Germany and retrieve the crucial element needed to revive their ailing leader, Jaja. Despite being confined to his sickbed, Jaja's presence loomed large in the coven. Though physically immobile, his reflective witchcraft projection sat stoically in his stead, a silent but potent reminder of his leadership.

The atmosphere crackled with energy as the assembled witches and wizards prepared to deliberate and decide the fate of their fraternity. Each member understood the gravity of the task at hand and the importance of their collective mission. As the meeting commenced, all eyes turned to the high chair where Jaja's projection sat, a symbol of resilience and determination in the face of adversity.

The spacious coven was a mysterious place; Brooms that were placed on their heads on the ground lined one side of the wall, half of which was covered with local mats, while rows of clay pots placed on plantain leaves and palm fronts lined the opposite end.

At the dark corner, the shadowy profile of a wizard hunched over the boiling magical preparation in the 'pot of life' which he was continuously stirring. All the witches and wizards were waiting for the final ingredient from Germany which they needed to complete the cocktail in the pot to aid the revitalization of the ailing leader.

On the floor, beside the 'pot of life' that was in the middle of three rocks and burning logs of wood, were stones. One of the agents of the ailing leader, who had the head of a broom bunch resting on top of his hat and an extra mouth on the palm of his right hand, had the impossible task of squeezing water out of the dry stones that were lying on the floor beside him, and this, he was doing with ease.

He would pick one from the stones and squeeze it letting the water drop into the pot. When he finished, he would pick up another stone from the floor and continue the process, while his partner kept stirring the content of the pot with a large wooden spoon and now and then, stopping to converse with the seven other stones with mouth and teeth that were laying on the ground beside him; Another sat beside him pounding some powdery substance in a mortal with a pestle.

Amidst the intense proceedings, a figure unlike any other materialized within the coven. A wizard, peculiar in appearance with a mouth sealed shut, hovered mysteriously in the air. But what caught everyone's attention was the additional mouth situated eerily in the centre of his right hand. With a dramatic gesture, he raised his hand, and from the unusual appendage, a gravelly voice echoed out, calling for the crowd's attention. "Opa ...Wa - ya-ya-ya-ya-ya-ya-ya!" the hand-mouth bellowed, its sound reverberating through the chamber.

"Wa – ya-ya-ya-ya-ya-ya-ya!" the crowd responded in unison, acknowledging the call.

With an ancient calabash brimming with a mysterious oil in hand, the enigmatic wizard floated above a pot simmering on the fire. With a fluid motion, he poured the fiery liquid into the pot, causing billows of steam to rise and fill the air with an intoxicating scent, mingled with the aroma of incense. Landing gracefully by the pot, he conjured a mirror and summoned forth an image of Jenny, eliciting cheers from the onlookers. Placing the mirror near the pot, he vanished into thin air as abruptly as he had arrived.

As anticipation mounted, the sceptre, symbolizing authority, and power, was reverently placed before the projection of the ailing leader. Elders paid homage to it with solemn "Opa!" chants, signifying their unwavering loyalty.

In due time, the selection of the acting leader commenced behind closed doors, with three candidates emerging as frontrunners. After careful deliberation, Sabon-Gari, the esteemed occult master, was unanimously chosen to assume the mantle of leadership. Adorned with a robe embellished with beads and presented with the sceptre, he received his mandate and was empowered to assemble a team for the crucial mission to retrieve the final element from Germany.

The coven was buzzing with eager anticipation ahead of the selection of the members of the team. It was the ultimate recognition of one's talent as a Weafric witch or wizard and an honour to be at the grand master's service and only the best was normally assigned. "This mission is not business as usual," said Sabon-Gari, as he was deliberating with the other leaders on the issue of picking the members of his team.

After careful consideration, the acting leader, who had risen rapidly through the ranks of the Weafric2w, finally picked the members of his team. Boniface, fondly called Koboko by his friends, was selected by the leader for his knack for creating unhappiness and suffering for others.

Also selected were the hard-hearted Mulumba from one of the East African countries, who was the head of the cup-bearer, and Malaika, the evil genius and the only female member of the group, who was the head of the witches, or Sangomas, in the Southern African region. She was well-known in the fraternity and her record as a wicked witch spoke volumes. "I like your impulse and that is why I'm bringing you into the team," the acting leader told her.

Toyosi was flushed with excitement at being selected to be part of the team. Looking at him, one would be mistaken to think he couldn't hurt a fly; His diminutive physique and innocent-looking face masked his cruel and vicious character. The wizard had always wanted to travel overseas and to show his talents on a bigger stage, and now, he felt he had the opportunity for something even bigger. After his selection, Toyosi capered about like a little lamb in enthusiasm.

Then the acting leader briefly addressed the members of his team.

"You've all been selected based on your track records," began the leader. "You all know this is a bigger responsibility than usual because it has to do with the life of our grandmaster and I hope you will be exemplary in the execution of the task," added the acting leader as he ended his speech. And then, with a stick, he touched each member of the team on the head and each of them subsequently pledged their allegiance to the leader.

As a child, Sabon-Gari was a force to be reckoned with, a turbulent soul whose presence stirred unease in his community. Born third in a brood of six, he was the unruliest among his siblings, earning himself a reputation for all things wicked. His father, a simple farmer, and his mother, a humble trader, rejoiced at his birth, particularly his mother, who had longed for a son after years of yearning.

But to the people of the village, Sabon-Gari was an enigma, a puzzle wrapped in mystery. His childhood was far from ordinary, marked by a profound disconnect from those around him. Communication was a struggle, and he shunned the company of other children, plagued by a deep-rooted insecurity.

Instead, he found solace in solitary places, wandering amidst the graves of the evil forest and the resting places of those believed to be touched by the supernatural, including infants who met untimely ends. His parents fretted over his peculiar behaviour, but their attempts to steer him away from his morbid fascination fell on deaf ears.

Sent to live with his grandmother in the village, Sabon-Gari's isolation only deepened. Alone in the eerie depths of the evil forest, he communed with spirits who nurtured and guided him, shaping his spiritual path.

As he matured, Sabon-Gari's presence cast a pall of fear over the village. Rarely seen without a menacing scowl, he became synonymous with occult practices and dark arts. His name evoked dread, a reminder of the pain and suffering he had inflicted upon the community.

Armed with a mystical diamond mirror, a sinister black chair, and unseen serpents, Sabon-Gari wielded powers beyond comprehension. His walking stick, a seemingly innocuous object, concealed a deadly secret, capable of transforming into a lethal serpent with a flick of his wrist. As the acting leader finalized his team, preparations began for the send-off celebration and farewell dance, marking the beginning of a perilous journey into the unknown.

Just then, one of the elderly albino wizards raised his hand and eyed the dancing drums that were lying in a corner; Suddenly, the four dancing drums stood erect and did obeisance to the wizard, and then, one after the other, each went flying in the air while making some dancing movements before finally resting in positions where bodiless-hand-drummers were waiting. Subsequently, the mortars and pestles started wriggling before making some dancing movements on the floor to their respective positions.

"Music!" ordered one of the albino wizards. Soon, the visible and invisible drummers started with a soothing, ethereal drum rhythm which soon developed and vibrated rhythmically with increasing intensity, swaying the entire crowd - save for the ailing leader, Jaja, who sat with impassive expression on his face.

Soon, the drummers and the dancers were in perfect synchrony. The dancers, clad in attires of sombre shades of grey and black danced exuberantly, gyrating and twisting to the pulsating rhythm of the drums, mortars and pestles that were pounded by the drummers who intermittently engaged in call sessions with their drums and the dancers responding with their dance steps and wild body movements as the witches sang, "Wale ! wale ! wale - wale - wale wale!" and the wizards responded, "Iya ! iya ! iya - iya - iya- iya!"

The atmosphere in the coven was electric as the dancers moved in perfect harmony, their bodies swaying to the pulsating rhythm of the drums. Some glided gracefully from side to side, while others leapt into the air with impressive agility, their feet tracing intricate patterns on the floor.

A group of four dancers caught everyone's attention as they spun and twisted with dizzying speed, their movements a mesmerizing blur of motion. Not to be outdone, another group showcased their energetic dance steps, their bodies moving in fluid motions as they smacked their foreheads with the palms of their hands, their spins resembling a spinning wheelbarrow.

Lucy, caught up in the fervour of the moment, joined the spectacle, her movements fluid and expressive. She danced towards the ailing grand master's projection, her body writhing in a symbolic gesture of reverence and supplication. Two other dancers, their bodies bent low to the ground, followed her lead, their movements mirroring her own.

Toyosi, the small but agile figure, threw himself into the dance with abandon. With eyes ablaze and face alight with excitement, he leaped into the fiery ring that adorned the floor, his movements quick and precise as he danced alongside the other witches.

As Queen observed the scene unfolding before her, her gaze shifted to the grand master, his figure a poignant reminder of the gravity of the situation. Despite his frail appearance and distant demeanour, he remained the focal point of the gathering, his presence a testament to his enduring strength.

The grand master's illness had taken its toll, leaving him weakened and vulnerable. Yet, there was hope in the form of Caddy, the blind old witch whose unwavering dedication provided a glimmer of optimism amidst the darkness.

Meanwhile, Sabon-Gari, now adorned in his ceremonial attire, infused the gathering with renewed energy as he danced with fervour. With each step, he seemed to channel the very essence of the drums, his movements a testament to his mastery of the craft.

Approaching the grand master with purpose, Sabon-Gari performed a series of intricate steps, his face alight with determination. With practised precision, he scooped a portion of the potion from the boiling pot, his movements fluid and confident as he prepared to administer the magic elixir. Holding the mirror containing Jenny's image aloft, and the calabash that contained the magic stuff in the other, he prepared to commence the final phase of the ritual.

Just then, three female dancers with three little dancing flames in the palms of their hands walked towards the leader and encircled him and one after the other they dropped their tongues of dancing flames on the mirror the leader was holding. Soon, the three tongues of flames came together as one big flame that continued dancing on the mirror that had Jenny's image and all those who were present bowed down their heads and chorused, "Opa... wa - ya-ya-ya-ya-ya-ya-ya!" And they did obeisance to the flame.

"Opa!" The leader called out, his eyes wide open, and the chatter of the drumming and singing voices suddenly quieted.

"We're going to Deutchland!" he announced.

"Hi - yah!" the crowd responded.

"To bring back the missing puzzle piece to revitalize our GM!" said the acting leader.

"Hi - yah!" the others answered.

"The Oyinbo girl with the golden hair!" added the acting leader, self-assuredly.

"Hi - yahhh!" the crowd chorused.

Sabon-Gari grinned widely and did a brief caper. After that, there was plenty of singing and dancing all through the night.

The next day, Lucy was in the presence of the acting leader who requested for Jenny's name and other information the former had obtained from the hotel where she worked. Jenny's data was then programmed into her image in the leader's special mirror so they could have direct access to her in their spiritual world.

Later in the day, Sabon-Gari telephoned his contact person, Koffo, who was a wizard and a member of the Weafric2w living in Germany. On the phone, the acting leader briefed him about developments back home and their proposed plan to visit Germany to complete the unfinished business of getting the last part of the essential ingredients needed to save the dying leader. "Since you've been living there for some time now, at least, you understand the terrain better than us," said the leader, "the blonde oyinbo girl is indispensable and, in fact, she's the only redeeming chance we must save our grand master. This is of paramount importance and the consequences of getting it wrong is not an option and simply don't bear thinking about which is why I personally will be heading the team," he added.

Koffo then promised to receive and guide the delegation when they arrived in Germany, while also promising to get team a serene environment as their base camp. First, he was going to send the leader a little video clip of their possible camp site - The Westfallen Park in Dortmund.

"And there are certain things I'd like to also discuss with you when we meet," said Koffo, who had a lot more on his mind.

"That's very nice of you," replied Sabon-Gari. "Having been living there for a while, I know you're familiar with the environment over there and understand the terrain better than any of us; So, you're going to be our eyes over there," added the acting leader.

"No problem!" replied Koffo. "You know, I'm one of you. Just let me know when the team is coming over and we'll arrange everything," he volunteered and hung up.

As promised, Koffo contacted Sabon-Gari four days later sending some pictures and a video clip with a brief description of the Westfallen Park in Dortmund, Germany. The witches and wizards were beside themselves with excitement as they got together to see the clip.

"This is Dortmund, the city the team could be staying in Germany, that is, if you like what you see." began the voice-over in the clip.

"Oh, Bloodmund! Bloodmund!" some of the wizards exclaimed and were excitedly whispering among themselves. The acting leader clapped his hands for silence and then paused the video clip.

"The city is not Bloodmund, but Dortmund," said the leader, who then let the film continue to run.

"Dortmund is a big, beautiful city of more than 700,000 inhabitants," the voice-over continued. "The city is known for nature, beautiful parks, and modern technology. It is situated in a much bigger area known as the Nordrhein -Westfalen. The first stroke of winter gives the park the look of a fairy-tale and this magnificent Westfalen Park could be your base, if you like it." The viewers gazed at the beautiful footage of the park that was being displaced on the screen.

"There are lots and lots of surprises for visitors to the park," continued the male voice in the clip. "The park has a Television tower from where one could have a superb panoramic view of a large section of the city of Dortmund. The park has halls for special events and accommodation facilities for both locals as well as foreigners all year round. The park has got children's programs and a museum as well as a specialized baker."

"Uhm!" Mulumba suddenly cut in.

"That's not all," the voice in the clip went on. "And, surprise, surprise! The park has got huts with thatched roofs like we have in many parts of our continent."

"Oi! So, they have these kinds of houses over there, too?" asked Toyosi.

Just then, the pictures of three huts, a grass-covered cottage and a strange enclosure looking like a pre-historic bird's nest that was built on a tree trunk were displayed on the screen.

"I'm going to stay in that one on the tree. I like it," said Malaika.

"In December," continued the voice-over in the clip, "Special lamps transform the park into a fairy-tale land. There are other features in the park, like a river where your boat could land when the team arrives. This is about the lot that forms some of the park's rich tapestry and how do you like it?"

When the video clip ended, all the witches and wizards clapped and cheered in approval. "Wao! Wao! We like it. We'll camp in this park!" they said.

Soon, the appointed day came for the trip to Germany. In the moments leading up to their departure, senior members of the Weafric2w community gathered on the tranquil shores of the river to bid farewell to the departing team. The atmosphere was charged with emotion as well-wishers offered words of encouragement and blessings to the travellers embarking on this important mission to the white man's land. There was a sense of camaraderie and solidarity among the gathered crowd, united in their support for the team and their shared commitment to the success of their endeavour.

Amidst the gentle lapping of the river against the shore, the departing team stood ready, their hearts filled with a mixture of anticipation and resolve. As they prepared to set sail for distant shores, they knew that they carried with them the hopes and aspirations of their community. With one final farewell, the team boarded their vessel and set off into the unknown, their journey ahead filled with promise and possibility. The Weafric witches and wizards had been playing roles in and far beyond their borders but never in the white men's territory. Now they were leaving their sphere of influence and they all felt this was going to be quite an exciting adventure.

"Sabon-Gari, the one who flies with one wing!" Babatunde, one of the most senior members of the fraternity and who had many folds and lines on the skin due to age, hailed the acting leader. "If you tasted something sweet, to lose it is painful. We have great confidence in you and your team to bring back the last element," he added.

"Thank you, Baba," replied Sabon-Gari. "What's lost can be found. I don't personally anticipate any problems getting the young lady. Though we're going to be sailing in uncharted waters, we'll bring her back." added the acting leader, with an air of confidence.

"Pearls and diamonds are covered and well protected in their natural settings. To find them, you must work hard and dig deep." Said Caddy, who gained prominence in the coven for her uncanny propensity for predicting improbable events years back. "The immediate future is clear, and I can see you succeeding in your important mission, but it is however hard to see what lies beyond that." continued the blind old witch who was still feeling a pang of regret that what they had under their wings a while ago was gone.

"My dear sister, Caddy, some things become clearer in the dark and sometimes we can see more with our eyes closed; By all means, we'll bring back the oyimbo girl and final solution to the jigsaw because she is a treasure of inestimable value and she already has our seal," replied Sabon-Gari, gently patting Caddy on the shoulder while simultaneously walking towards Mthembu, "With any luck we'll be in Germany before the day breaks, but if not, we'll stop over in Malta or Lampedussa. Ke nako! For the bond!" Said the acting leader, as he made his move to leave.

"For the bond! For the bond!" the others responded and wished the team success on their important mission. They were well equipped for the journey, but Mthembu checked once again to ensure the team had not forgotten anything that was needed - Emergency parachutes, sleeping bags, magic brooms, a map, pairs of binoculars and special navigational tools.

Sabon-Gari and his team made their way toward a marvel of technology unlike anything seen before - the 9-seater revolutionary flying Boat that was known in Niani as the Boatplane. This medium-sized, purpose-built craft represented the pinnacle of Weafric2w's ingenuity and innovation and stood as one of the most advanced in their smart eco-range, medium-sized stealth vehicles tailored for long-distance travel.

The Boatplane's design was nothing short of extraordinary. It possessed the remarkable ability to traverse various air defence systems undetected, a feat achieved through a combination of cutting-edge technology and mystical craftsmanship. While modern stealth aircraft typically evade detection by microwave radar, the Boatplanes from Nogokpo took stealth to a whole new level, remaining invisible even to high-frequency beams—a phenomenon that defied conventional physics and underscored the Weafric2w's mastery of engineering.

Constructed through a process known as mystique reverse engineering, these seemingly simple yet highly sophisticated aerial boats represented the height of operational intelligence. Equipped with both advanced infrared sensors and the super-active lean technology, they could adjust their sizes to carry more than their normal capacity, and autonomously detect and navigate obstacles when being used as normal boats, adapting seamlessly to the pilot's commands. Their intuitive controls, linked to magical brooms, allowed for precise manoeuvring in both horizontal and vertical directions.

Inside, the Boatplane resembled a miniature mobile lounge, boasting creature comforts akin to those found in luxury aircraft. Its sleek, aerodynamically sculpted exterior was crafted from cellulose-based wood and specially modified wysips crystals that could harness the sun's rays during the day to generate electric energy stored in super capacitors. Alternatively, some models utilized an electrolyte flow cell power system to drive their engines.

Among the controls were knobs linked to two satellite dishes positioned at the rear of the Boat. These dishes, slightly larger than teacup saucers, were crafted from specially treated cobwebs sourced from remote jungles inhabited by giant spiders. Extending above the rims were feed cones electromagnetically connected to ground control antennas located in the heart of Nogokpo, ensuring seamless communication with the outside world.

In addition to the propellant extraordinary brooms secured in the centre of the dashboard, the cockpit housed an array of contraptions crafted by Nogokpo's finest scientists and engineers. A smart television set and an in-built calabash provided access to live visuals of Mulumba's colleagues on the shore. Flexing their creativity, the engineers had incorporated a dozen flexible, coloured hollow nails with glass-topped heads, each transmitting different signals.

Alongside these innovations, the dashboard featured specially treated broomsticks and transparent metal leaves, intricately engineered to contain microchips and nano-substances. Specially modified leaf buds emitted soft light from translucent roots, while bio-luminescent insects and worms inhabited transparent encased vases, adding to the ethereal atmosphere.

One particularly intriguing feature was a stone with teeth, emitting flashing neon lights from its open mouth. Positioned above the dashboard's mirror and held in place by metallic threads spun from cobwebs, it added a touch of whimsy to the Boat's interior. Overall, the interior of the Boat seamlessly blended technological innovation with natural elements, reflecting the ingenuity and creativity of Ni´s brightest minds.

Before boarding, Mulumba, one of Nogokpo´s experienced pilots, had conducted a quick check to ensure the craft's readiness for flight. The pilot leaned forward, his fingers delicately tapping the array of knobs and coloured broomsticks that adorned the Boat's cockpit. The control panel, integrated seamlessly into the full-length interactive dashboard, boasted wood-themed features and an entertainment system. This sophisticated digital interface responded to the pilot´s touch, hand gestures and eye movements.

As Mulumba adjusted the knobs, the interior of the Boat sprang to life. High-intensity incandescent lamp bulbs, containing xenon, krypton, and neon gas, illuminated overhead, casting vivid colours and complex patterns throughout the cabin. Meanwhile, rows of twinkling mini capsules of lights lined the interior, creating an enchanting ambience. "Lady and gentlemen, you're welcome on board.

This is your flight Captain, Mulumba, speaking. In a few minutes, we'll be airborne. Please, fasten your seat belts, sit back, relax, and enjoy the comfort of our Boatcraft. Wishing you a pleasant flight!" Announced the pilot.

When he had finished speaking, Toyosi and Malaika chuckled amusingly. Sabon-Gari momentarily raised his head from the map he was looking at, stole a glance at the flight Captain and then smiled. It was a great privilege to pilot one of these advanced machines and the leader was extremely proud of Mulumba. All was now set for the team to take off and most of them were feeling tinges of excitement and anticipation.

As departure time approached, the pilot carefully detached one of the computer-aided propellant magical brooms from its firm fixture on the dashboard. Each stick of the broom was equipped with sensors that controlled the engine unit, ensuring precise navigation. With a gentle touch akin to operating a remote control, he tapped the soft glass-topped head of a green flexible nail, initiating the vehicle's movement.

As the boat glided sideways and then forward away from the shore, the pilot manipulated a knob inside a small metallic flower linked to the Boat's sophisticated coding system. With deft movements, he adjusted the petals while tilted the flower back and forth, his eyes focused intently on the screen of the television set displaying binary numbers, AI algorithms, and encrypted messages understood by only a select few.

Slowly, the cabin cruiser rose above the waters of the river, momentarily hovering in the air before ascending vertically, gaining altitude with each passing moment. After attaining the right altitude, the pilot swirled his propellant magical broom in a forward motion. Responding to the broom's movement, the artificial intelligence-enabled boat began to glide noiselessly, its ascent graceful as it tilted upwards, climbing steadily to its cruising altitude.

Meanwhile, just as the boat was lifting above the waters of the river, Boniface broke into a tune and soon the others joined him as they all chorused the modified nursery lines:

> Row, row, row your boat.
>
> Row, row, row your boat.
>
> Down to Germany
>
> Merrily. merrily, merrily, merrily
>
> To get the German lady
>
> To get the German lady
>
> The girl with the golden hair.

And then, with a powerful surge of speed, the boat shot off into the night sky, leaving behind the familiar landscape.

Chapter 5

The Mission

The journey for the Weafric2w team to Germany lasted just over five hours, during which the GPS-tagged stealth super Boat-plane glided effortlessly through the sky. Sabon-Gari, in constant communication with special agents back in Nogokpo, ensured a smooth flight. As they approached their destination, the pilot switched the cruise control to manual, meticulously determining the optimal landing position.

Hovering above Westfalen Park in Dortmund, the craft delicately adjusted its position before slowly descending towards the serene waters below. With precision, it touched down just before 5 am local time. Almost immediately, a message appeared on one of the mirrors on the craft's dashboard: "Wishing you and the team a successful mission!" It was a reassuring note from their base in Nogokpo.

After confirming their safe arrival with a radio signal to base, the pilot expertly navigated the Boat-plane to a secluded spot behind a canopy of trees along the water's edge, concealing their arrival. With a sense of accomplishment, the pilot declared, "Germany, here we come!"

Koffo was on hand to receive the delegation. "Sabon-Sabon! Sabon-Sabon! Sabon-Gari himself!" Koffo hailed the leader and did obeisance to him as they disembarked and stepped onto solid ground. Sabon-Gari's face cracked into a smile. "You're all welcome! For the bond!" said Koffo.

"For the bond!" the others replied heartily, as they shook hands and exchanged pleasantries.

"How was the trip?" asked Koffo.

"Oh, it was wonderful! The trip was made easy by the comfort of our speedy new model Boat. How nice to set a foot on your soil!" replied the leader trying to conceal his smile.

"On my soil? Haba, my boss, you're in Deutschland, the home of the Germans; You're all welcome to Germany!" said Koffo, who was quite joyous to link up with the team and he soon mixed up with the members some of whom he last met more than three years ago.

"By the way, this machine looks gorgeous and wicked!" remarked Koffo, who had not seen this model of the Flying Boats.

"Ah, you mean, our new Boatroplane?" Asked Mulumba.

"Yes, this machine you have here, it looks super!" answered Koffo.

"Oh, that's the latest piece of engineering and our new anomalous type of water and aircraft in Nogokpo." Said Mulumba. "It is built with a special unconventional form of propulsion, like the positive lift that defies the laws of aerodynamics, and it can manoeuvre in ways that include extreme manoeuvrability beyond the normal g-forces of modern aircraft," added the pilot.

"Really? Wao, that sounds fantastic!" replied Koffo.

After a brief period of relaxation, Malaika, showing some initial signs of jet lag, quickly shook off her travel fatigue. Koffo and Mulumba proceeded to properly conceal the boat plane with leaves, ensuring it remained hidden from prying eyes. With the craft safely tucked away, they embarked on a stroll through Westfallen Park, eager to immerse themselves in their new surroundings.

Guided by Koffo, they explored the park, finding it just as idyllic as they had seen in the video clip he had shared. They aimed to familiarize themselves with the area before settling in for the next few days. They came across a quaint cottage adorned with grass and creeping plants, emanating a serene ambience. Nearby, they discovered rustic huts, each team member selecting their preferred accommodation. Sabon-Gari was captivated by the charm of the cottage, while Malaika opted for a unique hut constructed from latticed woodwork and perched atop a tree trunk.

After the team had settled down, the Chef de mission briefly interfaced with the members, "First, I would like to thank our brother Koffo for the warm reception. I can say that this park is excellent! The surrounding river and the forest are natural and marvellous! I hope as a team we will all work together to accomplish our mission here." said Sabon-Gari, who was aware they were now out of their normal orbit and in a different time zone. "You all know why we're here and I expect good conduct from every one of you. You should beware of doing or saying anything that could reveal who you are or jeopardize our mission. Just blend in and don't do anything to draw any undue attention" he counselled.

The following day greeted them with warm sunshine as they embarked on a tour of Dortmund's city centre, riding a clanging tram through its bustling streets. Koffo led the excursion, showcasing the city's architectural wonders while offering insights into local customs and culture. By evening, some members of the team were fatigued from the day's activities and retired to bed early.

Sabon-Gari awoke the next morning to the distant, throaty howl of Boniface, echoing through the midnight air. This familiar sound, akin to an owl's hoot, served as a unique announcement of Boniface's presence. Sabon-Gari, accustomed to this ritual, greeted the dawn with a sense of familiarity and readiness for the day ahead.

At this moment, the leader wanted to telepathically communicate with Jenny, and it wasn't difficult for him to locate her as they already had her in their spiritual radar, and through the invisible mark with the coded information on her forehead, he could always open a line of communication with her whenever he wanted. By means of remote sensing, he plugged and called up Jenny's image in his divination calabash and was secretly observing her activities. The leader could also see that the family had got an extraordinary cat.

A few hours later, Koffo paid a visit to his colleagues in the Westfalen Park to set out their plans. After their discussions, he proposed to treat the team with some African food at his house later in the day. For breakfast that morning, the team decided to visit one of the restaurants in the park and order some food. While they were eating, Boniface unintentionally caused a stir when he shoved the utensils on the table aside and was eating with his bare hands to the amusement of some of the other guests in the restaurant. "Back home, some local dishes were traditionally eaten without cutlery, why not in Germany?" he thought.

Sabon-Gari looked at Boniface disapprovingly.

"Boniface, what are you doing?" asked the leader.

"Ah-ah, I'm eating, of course!" answered the latter.

"Didn't I say no theatrics? Can't you see you're the odd one out here? asked the embarrassed leader in a low tone, while looking at the cutlery on the table. Boniface gave a smile of dry amusement, then raised his head and looked around. He noticed that some of the other diners were amused seeing him eating with his bare fingers and were watching him.

Subsequently, Boniface stretched his hands over the utensils on the table and muttered some magic words and the fork and knife suddenly sprang from the table and into his outstretched hands, as though, the wizard had magnetic hands, this he did with a touch of a little drama to entertain the two little kids who were sitting with their parents at the far end of the large dining room – And then, Boniface continued with his food.

Later in the day, as darkness fell across Deutchland and the rest of the country was fast asleep, the witching hour to act was getting close at hand. The team of African wizards and the witch were in an upbeat mood and filled with a sense of anticipation as they assembled at their leader's cottage to prepare for their mission.

"Ke nako!" said Sabon-Gari.

"Ke nako!" replied the others.

Although, that afternoon, the leader who had been remotely viewing Jenny and had already programmed their destination in his unconventional satellite navigation system, however, asked Koffo who was already used to the terrain to lead the way as they grabbed their brooms and headed towards Hexenburg.

As they reached Jenny's residence nestled on a tranquil residential street, Sabon-Gari carefully assessed the surroundings before springing into action. With precision, he instructed Toyosi, Mulumba, and Malaika to remain outside while the rest of the team transformed into rats, squeezing through the narrow gap beneath the securely locked main door. Once inside, they swiftly reverted to their human forms.

Sabon-Gari led the way, navigating through the house until he reached Jenny's room. There, amidst the silence, Jenny lay sound asleep, unaware of the impending intrusion. With practised ease, Sabon-Gari entered her room, his movements calculated and deliberate, while Koffo and Boniface remained vigilant in the sitting room, keeping watch for any signs of activity from the household.

However, just as they began their clandestine mission, an unexpected obstacle emerged in the form of the family cat. Sensing the presence of unfamiliar figures, the feline intruder wandered into Jenny's room, casting an air of tension over the operation. It warily eyed the leader who was standing in a corner. That was no ordinary cat, Sabon-Gari knew that and had come prepared with a secret weapon.

The leader hunched his shoulders thrusting his hand deep into his pocket and pulled out his secret weapon against the mysterious cats.

"When a cat sees a lion, it is bound to retreat... Chaubun-nagun-ga-mugg!" he muttered and threw the object on the floor.

As the cat cautiously approached the unfamiliar object lying on the floor, adorned with feathers that seemed to dance in the faint light, its curiosity piqued. With delicate movements, it inched closer, hoping to engage in a playful encounter akin to its past interactions with Petra's beloved ball of wool. However, as its whiskers twitched, detecting an unusual scent emanating from the object, a sense of unease began to creep over the feline.

Suddenly, the cat's pupils dilated, reflecting the dim light with an eerie glow as it registered the peculiar aroma wafting from the object. Sensing danger lurking within its midst, the cat's instincts kicked into high gear, propelling it into swift motion. With a startled yowl, it darted across the floor, its claws skittering against the surface as it made a beeline for Petra's comforting presence atop the bed.

Joining Petra in a flurry of movement, the cat sought solace in the familiar warmth of her embrace, its heart still racing from the unnerving encounter with the enigmatic object.

"Are you okay, my darling?" She asked, as she cuddled the cat softly, and did not suspect that danger was lurking in the house.

Smiling mysteriously, Sabon-Gari, the diabolical genius, cast a furtive glance at Jenny who was fast asleep on her bed, then walked up to her and whispered, "Hello, my precious jewel." He sprayed some powder on Jenny before producing a black handkerchief from his pocket. "Chau-bun...a-gung...ga-mugg!" he chanted in a whispering tone and wiped Jenny's face with it.

The occult master then carried Jenny from the bed and placed her on her feet. Then, he used his magic to properly position her sleeping but hypnotized body to maintain an upright balance. That done, he proceeded to transform Jenny's appearance which he did quickly in different stages.

"Oyinbo mwanamke...kuja! Charrrgogg-agogg, Manchau-gagogg, Chaubun-nagun-gamugg!" he intoned, and then transformed the young lady into a pocket-sized human, small enough to fit into the little wooden box he specifically brought for the purpose. With the transformation completed, Sabon-Gari carefully carried and placed the miniaturized Jenny inside the little box and stealthily left the room along with the others. Having taken possession of their prized treasure, the team left Hexenburg and flew back to their base in Dortmund.

At Westfalen Park, the members of the Weafric2w were buzzing with excitement and congratulating themselves on having succeeded in their mission - getting Jenny had been a lot easier than they had envisaged. "You've all done very well!" Sabon-Gari commended his team.

Meanwhile, that night after the departure of the team of African wizards and the witch with Jenny under their wings, the family cats began to meow cryptically. Petra, who could read the cats' feelings intuitively sensed that something was amiss. She stepped out of bed to check things out in the house, then she discovered that Jenny was not in her room. She informed her husband, and they searched in and around the house for her, but she was nowhere to be found. Her disappearance left the family in shock and horror and the parents were beside themselves with worry and could no longer sleep that night.

"But Jenny slept on this bed just hours ago. I didn't hear any of the doors open and nobody broke in," said Dieter.

"Everything appears weird!" answered Petra. "Jenny has her key to the house and here is her key on the bunch on the table. How could Jenny leave the house at this hour of the night without informing anybody?" she asked, walking in the dreamy way of someone in a state of shock towards the sofa in the sitting room. They were both baffled by the situation but decided to wait till morning before informing the police, as it was possible Jenny could return from wherever she had gone.

In the morning, when they still couldn't find Jenny, Dieter called the police to report the case. Moments later, three police officers arrived to take photographs of the scene as well as to obtain statements from the couple. "A child going missing is one of a parent's worst nightmares." said one of the officers as his colleagues were taking pictures and searching for fingerprints, DNA, and other incriminating evidence.

"Her disappearance is completely out of character as she has never gone missing before," replied Petra.

"We are equally concerned about her safety," said the police officer, "and I can assure you that all available search assets will be used to find her," he assured. The family thanked the officers.

When the police had left, Petra telephoned Ursula, the school's director to relate the unsettling news.

"Something strange happened last night. Jenny mysteriously disappeared from the house, and we haven't been able to find her," said Petra drearily on the phone.

"That's very strange! Where could she have gone without informing any member of the family?" asked Ursula.

"I don't know, everything's still a mystery to us," replied Petra.

"Have you alerted the police yet?" asked Ursula.

"Yes, they were here not long ago and promised to do all they could to find her," replied Petra, who was becoming too distraught to speak about the tragedy and desperately trying to fight back the tears that were welling up in her eyes.

"Don't worry, my dear, I'm sure everything will be alright! Said Ursula reassuringly. Just exercise some patience and confidence in allowing the police to do their work; Wait for me at home, I'm coming to you right away." Added Ursula.

The news of Jenny's sudden disappearance sent shockwaves rippling through the tight-knit community surrounding the school where Petra was employed. As word spread like wildfire, a palpable sense of disbelief and concern permeated the air, leaving teachers and students alike grappling with a multitude of unanswered questions.

In the staff room, murmurs of disbelief and concern filled the air as colleagues exchanged worried glances and whispered conversations. "How could something like this happen?" echoed through the room, each voice tinged with a mixture of disbelief and apprehension.

Outside the school gates, Bearbel and Jorg, the immediate neighbours of Jenny's family, arrived with furrowed brows and sympathetic expressions, eager to offer their support in any way they could. As the news continued to reverberate throughout the neighbourhood, anxious relatives and concerned members of the local community began to gather, drawn together by a shared sense of solidarity and compassion for the distraught family. Amidst the sombre atmosphere, gestures of kindness and empathy served as a beacon of hope amidst the uncertainty, as friends, neighbours, and strangers alike rallied around the family in their time of need, united in their determination to support and comfort them through the ordeal.

Meanwhile, back in Westfalen Park the next morning, an excited Sabon-Gari decided to break the news of their successful mission to his colleagues back home.

"Is that Babatunde?" asked Sabon-Gari, on the phone line to Nigeria.

"Yes, I 'm right on the line ... ah, that sounds like Sabon himself!" replied Babatunde, who, together with the others, had been anxiously waiting to know about the team's progress on their mission.

"Good day, Baba, I've some piece of good news for you!" Sabon-Gari declared excitedly. "We've taken possession of the treasure! Our GM will get over this!" added the leader, grinning with delight.

"You mean you've got the girl?" asked Babatunde.

"Who else? Yes, of course!" replied Sabon-Gari, with a note of triumph in his voice.

"That's great news! And this is a great moment for us!" said Babatunde excitedly. "You know, my dear, I did not doubt that the spider's web would catch the fly; You've done tremendously well! So, when are you coming back with the jewel?" he asked.

"Oh, soon … as soon as possible. I'll give you a call when we're ready to leave," answered the acting leader in a rare sign of exuberance.

"That's good! You and the team will get the warm welcome you deserve, and we shall make great arrangements for your reception and throw the biggest party our land has ever seen! Please, you must make it quick. You know how urgent this is for our GM," said Babatunde.

"Oh yes, I know! We'll be back home soon. For the bond!" replied Sabon-Gari.

"For the bond!" Babatunde responded and hung up. There were smiles and hugs all around when Babatunde broke the news of the team's accomplishment to his fellows.

Later in the day, Koffo was in the Westfalen Park to discuss with Sabon-Gari. This was something they couldn't discuss on the phone. "What I'm about to tell you is a golden opportunity for us to kill two birds with one stone, and we have already killed one of the birds." began Koffo, after settling down in their leader's little cottage. "This is something I've always wanted to tell our grandmaster and the other leaders but have refrained from doing because I know that the majority of them are against the idea of introducing our technology for our regional development." Koffo paused trying to measure the leader's reaction.

"I'm listening," said Sabon-Gari.

"You know, I've been living here for a while," continued Koffo. "I believe it is within our powers to recreate in our world the technological wonders that we see all around us today. Now, our leaders are reluctant to introduce Nogokpo's technological ideas to develop our real world and if we're not allowed to use what we must get what we want back home, we can, as well, use our powers to get some of their hi-tech here in Germany, as things are more open down here." he submitted.

"Um-hum, so, what are you driving at?" asked Sabon-Gari.

"I'm suggesting we use the opportunity of our physical presence here in Germany to get our hands on some German technology. I believe we can use our powers to acquire some of their industrial secrets," said Koffo.

"Sounds interesting," replied Sabon-Gari. Then the leader added, "But you know as well as I do that, we have all that we need in our territory. Now tell me, what use do we have for cars or aeroplanes when we can get from point A to point B without any stress? On the scientific and technological front, we are not far behind either, and in fact, we're pacesetters and ahead of the Western world in many areas as our scientists have developed anti-stealth radar from the spider web and other scientific breakthroughs – This is not the stuff of science fiction, but science fact. You know very well that things are not difficult for us in Nogokpo and I wonder why you are now complaining. Or have they indoctrinated you into their system here?"

"Opa, I see what you mean," replied Koffo. "But that is in our realm and of what use is technology if the discoveries can't be translated and used in the real world? Furthermore, we can aim for new frontiers. We can generally redirect our powers, talents, and craft like they do in the West. How long must we continue to take the back seat in the international community of witches?" asked Koffo, while taking a brief pause and then continuing, "The wizards here have been able to develop and organize their craft and powers to perform physical, technological, and scientific wonders and that's why whenever our local wizards come here, they quickly develop their potentials and thus perform better. This is reality, I live here among them and can see everything. You cannot compare our standards of operation back home to what is obtained here in Germany."

"So, what are you suggesting? That our craft is second-rate?" asked the leader coldly, raising his voice and looking straight into Koffo's eyes.

"Oh, no, far from it, Opa!" answered Koffo. "I'm not in any way downgrading or disrespecting our craft. On the contrary, I believe it's phenomenal what the scientists of Nogokpo are doing. But Opa, you'll agree with me that we, as the Weafric wizards, can only give what we're allowed to give, and so, we cannot go beyond our abilities. The only way forward now is either to open things up back home and convert our ideas in Nogokpo to transform our real world by showing the world or should I say the West, our hidden wonders and bringing our craft and experience to a larger theatre of expression or in the absence of that, take such knowledge from those who have invested in their craft to produce the things we enjoy today in the physical world," Koffo counselled.

"This is partly why I came here to Germany to be abreast with modern witchcraft. But the truth is, these people aren't eager to share their deep secrets, which is why I'm now suggesting stealing some of these secrets to aid the development of our region. We can make it happen in our world, and I believe it can happen under your leadership. You can make use of this opportunity faith has placed on your shoulders as a new leader by breaking the mould." added Koffo, his voice measured and calm, taking on the credence of a preacher.

Upon hearing that, Sabon-Gari smiled. "Koffo. I've heard you." replied the acting leader. "You know that our means forbid us from indulging in such ideas and delightful fantasies like you're proposing to me. Furthermore, you should be very careful not to act against our age-old tradition, the consequences of which you're aware," he added.

After Koffo had left, Sabon-Gari was in the solitude of his cottage in the evening and thought long and hard about the young man's proposal to him. He reflected on Koffo's words that they had the power to get whatever they wanted in Germany.

"Uhm... there's some sense in Koffo's proposal, and a successful outcome of his ideas isn't beyond the realms of possibility. After all, we've accomplished our main mission and we've got nothing to lose, but rather, much to gain if we could lay our hands on some vital German technological secrets to add to what we've got back home." the wizard muttered to himself and his face suddenly brightened as he stirred at the picture of a section of the Westfalen Park that was hanging on the wall.

"And, come to think of it, will I not be making history to be the first Weafric leader to attempt to translate our wizardry in Nogokpo to the physical world of our region? After all, that's exactly what our counterparts in the Western world are doing... uhm, it makes perfect sense! Who knows where that young man's ideas would lead us?" the leader again muttered to himself with a distant dreamy look in his eyes.

Sabon-Gari ruminated over the issue that night and decided to speak with Koffo again the next day to learn more. At the back of his mind, the leader knew he'd have a hard time convincing the members of his team, and, more importantly, the elders and the other die-hard leaders back home who by long tradition, were already accustomed to set of protocols and strongly oppose change and, how was he going to sell the idea to them anyway? "Uhm...that's a tough nut!" he thought. Nevertheless, he'd resolved to give Koffo's proposal a try. "How truly wonderful it would be to reproduce some of the technological wizardry of the Germans and combine that with ours!" he thought to himself.

In the morning the next day, Sabon-Gari invited Koffo to his cottage.

"You know, Koffo, I thought about your proposal to me yesterday." the leader began. "I'd like to say that even though I find your ideas interesting, I think, it may not be practical because of the risk potentials. I've also been wondering how the others back home in Niani, the city of impossibilities, would receive..."

"Impossibilities, yes, with the exception, of course, of our inability to find a cure to our GM's ailment!" cut in Koffo.

"Ah... yeah, but that's why we're here." Replied Sabon-Gari.

"Opa, you know, it has been said that if there's ever going to be a change in anything, the minds of men must first be fitted to it. For many years, our great craft has mostly been underground and without any real substance or relevance in the physical world of our region; Yes, I know that most, if not all, of our leaders in the fraternity, oppose change and the introduction of our wonderful ideas in Niani to the physical world of our region for the world to appreciate, but I've always known you to be different. We can begin from here to challenge old models and be ready to do things differently. Now, I believe, we can set about a complete change of our static ideology and begin the practice of progressive witchcraft. Your new position as acting leader provides a unique opportunity to inspire this historic change and make a difference. This is our time, it's either we move forward or continue with more of the same, the choice is ours." he averred.

"Koffo, you've spoken well," replied Sabon-Gari. "I, too, feel that we need to begin to properly re-orientate ourselves in a new direction, particularly, the leadership of the brotherhood, for our collective progress. But you know it is crucially important that we get everything right. I'd like to hear the fine details of your proposal." said the leader.

Koffo then went on to elaborate on his plans of them using their magical powers to secretly steal sensitive information from the computers of some top German business organizations.

"I have three of the biggest tech giants here in mind," said Koffo "The first is Gilde Meister, a mechanical engineering company based in Bielefeld, that specializes in producing machines that produce other machines. The other is Siemens, whose big office here is in München, in Bayern. Siemens is one of the largest electrical, electronics and engineering companies that specializes in telecommunications in the world. One of Siemens' biggest businesses is selling industrial control systems. The third is the biggest automobile company here, or we could go for a mining company if you wish" he explained.

"That sounds very interesting!" replied Sabon-Gari.

"Opa, we'll have a glorious future ahead of us if we can lay our hands on the secret data of these firms!" declared Koffo with a sly grin.

After lunch, Sabon-Gari and Koffo met, they discussed and fine-tuned their plans before contacting the other members of the team to deliberate on the latter's proposal. "My brothers and sister, I'm sure you all know that Germany is a country renowned for its technology." began Sabon-Gari. "Following my observations here since our arrival, it has positively struck me how we could use Western technology to improve our lives and bring real development and progress to our people and region. Having accomplished our mission here by picking up the last piece of the puzzle to save our GM, we have no other challenges; I've decided it would be a bonus for the team to stay a few more days to wrap things up as icing on our cake by acquiring some technological secrets from here to surprise them back home." added the leader, pausing to assess the reaction of those he was addressing.

There was palpable surprise written on the others' faces as they listened to their leader. Most of them could not understand what had come over their leader because of his sudden change of attitude. It was taboo to speak of progress and development in their world and, thus, they were shocked that their no-nonsense leader who was known to be opposed to change was now speaking in such terms.

"Ehn... Mulumba, did you hear that? Progress... development... in our region..." whispered Boniface to his colleague, who was sitting beside him.

"Progress? What progress?" asked Mulumba quizzically. "This is unbelievable! I feel like breaking his neck, right away!" he added in a hushed tone.

"Opa, with due respect, I think your proposal is against our rules and it 'll not work," said Boniface. "And how can you begin to do something if you don't even believe in it in the first instance?" he asked.

"Yes! Yes!" concurred Mulumba. "A tree will always produce its kind. Moreover, you cannot break the mould and our centuries-old tradition just like that." He continued.

"And, ultimately Opa, you know that your proposal and ideas will require the stamp of the general council," added Boniface.

"Boniface, I know how you feel," replied Sabon-Gari calmly. "I'm also very much aware of our rules and traditions and we are governed and limited by what we can and can't do and while we are not ready yet to showcase our city, Nogokpo, to the rest of the world, we cannot however continue to allow our development and progress to be restricted by rules and conventions. At some certain point in time, things have got to change. When we get back home, I'm going to push for that change, the change of our restrictive policies, and the first step starts from here. For now, I have resolved to work with you all to bring about this change." added the leader.

"Oh, that sounds good! I smell glory!" said Malaika, clasping the bracelet around her wrist. Then she added, "I'm strongly in support of your proposal because it has the potential of transforming the lives of millions of people - making some a lot of money... and leaving behind others who don't want to change. I think we need to be more outward-looking, and I am open for business."

"Yes, you're right, Malaika." cut in Toyosi. "Opa, you're a rare breed to have conceived such an idea. You know, this could be our doorway to success and... ehm...progress. The world is constantly evolving, and we must move with the time," said the small man. And then, looking at Boniface in the eye, he continued, "If you don't want to move forward with us, then, you still want to be going analogue and that is old school; But now, we're going digital. I have a feeling that we could be giants a few years down the road if we can handle this very well."

"Giants indeed!" retorted Mulumba. "I'm rather surprised that you're all talking like this. Remember, we came here with a clear mission to get the last element for the sake of our GM - why, now, have some of you decided to change the plan?" he asked.

"Our mission hasn't changed!" interjected Sabon-Gari. "Why are you questioning me? Am I not your leader?" he asked, looking at Mulumba quizzically. "Now let me ask you, isn't it about time we changed our names as agents of retrogression? Isn't it time we changed the perception about us as enemies of progress to real partners of progress? I believe that laying our hands on some German industrial secrets in addition to what we have at home won't kill us, rather it will bring about a huge metamorphosis that will lead to a brighter, rewarding future for every one of us and our region." continued the leader.

"Opa, I'm with you," said Malaika. "Truly the world today is dominated by technology as never before. It is impossible to travel anywhere without seeing the manifestations of technological wizardry which has shaped life on our planet today," she added.

"My dear, Boniface, I know that you have a deep distrust of modern technology, and I can also understand your fears and objection to bringing a change to a system that has never been disrupted." Koffo, who had been silently listening to the discussion with keen interest finally opened. "You all know that I have been living in Germany for some time now and I'm not unfamiliar with the flow of things here. You cannot give what you don't have and, you know, everything in our world today has gone scientific," continued Koffo. "The people who have moved it this far are the Europeans and the Americans. It is in the West that you have all the innovations in modern science and technology, medicine et cetera because they set the trend and their approach to witchcraft is scientific.

It's a serious business and we must embrace change or become stagnant and there's so much we can learn from the white witches." Koffo posited and paused to gauge the feelings of his colleagues.

"And while they have long found the answers to the transfer of technology from the spiritual to their physical world, we, on our part, are still groping in the dark due to lack of the political will from our leaders in Niani to allow the transfer of our know-how to the physical world of our region to let the world see our capabilities and wonders. Our engineers are among the best, but we're yet to show this to the world." He paused. And then continued, "I hope you all can see what I see. Now the change we crave is coming because no institution resists the laws of circles and change. You can't stop change; you can't stop something that works. I'm so pleased that our leader here has agreed to pilot the idea, and I want to finally add that the deeds that we do today are the deeds that will echo throughout our land." Koffo finally submitted.

"This is no longer going to be business as usual," said Sabon-Gari. "We've realized and now understand how real development can take place and I'm challenging every one of you to play your role for the bond," he added.

"Yes, for the bond!" said Koffo in agreement.

"For the bond!" cut in Malaika.

"We have the powers to do anything. If you have a hammer in your hands, every problem should look like a nail. For the bond and the sake of our progress!" enthused Toyosi, who had by now climbed the tree and positioned himself upside down, while gently rocking from side to side with his bent knee clutching one of the tree branches.

"Opa, all that you desire, I'm willing to do for the bond," said Boniface.

"Count me in. For the bond!" added Mulumba. The Weafric witches and wizards highly valued their common bond which was the union and their desire to advance their mutual strategic interests.

After this, Koffo was asked to throw more light on the plans and the other members of the team subsequently discussed the specifics of the former's proposition.

For Koffo, it was a now-or-never opportunity to try to realize what he always had in mind. He was pleased with himself for managing to convince the other members of the team to work with him to carry out his plans. Even if they eventually succeeded in their secret mission of obtaining the industrial secrets, Koffo, like Sabon-Gari, was aware of the challenging task of selling their new ideas to the others back home. "That would be taken care of when the time comes," he muttered to himself. Now his first main task was to obtain the computer passwords of the various companies they would be targeting.

When Koffo returned home that evening, a sense of determination fuelled his late-night endeavours as he meticulously fine-tuned his intricate plans. The following morning, under the cloak of darkness, he arrived at the Gilde Meister premises in Bielefeld, a sense of anticipation mingling with the chill morning air.

Surveying the industrial estate with a cautious eye, Koffo found himself alone amidst the looming shadows, a solitary figure in the dimly lit landscape. With a deft flick of his wand, he transformed into a tiny mouse, the perfect disguise to evade the watchful gaze of surveillance cameras as he slipped through the unguarded gate.

Once inside the Chief Mechanical Engineer's office, Koffo strategically positioned his magic mirror on a nearby shelf before seamlessly melding into the shadows, his form barely discernible within the narrow confines of the shelving unit. From this vantage point, he patiently awaited the Engineer's arrival, his keen senses attuned to the faintest stirrings of activity below.

Hours passed in silence, the only sound was the soft rustle of papers and the occasional click of a mouse. Then, as the door swung open, Koffo held his breath as Bernd, the Chief Engineer, entered the room, the weight of his presence palpable in the stillness of the office.

With practised ease, Koffo observed as Bernd settled at his desk, the glow of the computer screen casting an ethereal light across the room. Moments later, the telltale click-clack of keys filled the air as Bernd entered his proprietary password, unaware of the watchful eyes trained upon him.

Like a silent sentinel, Koffo remained hidden, his focus unwavering as he committed the password to memory, every detail etched into his mind's eye. As the day ended, Koffo slipped away undetected, his mission accomplished.

In the days that followed, Koffo repeated this clandestine dance, obtaining passwords from the other marked companies with the precision of a master thief. With each success, he relayed the vital information to Sabon-Gari, laying the groundwork for their covert operation.

However, when the time came to put their plan into action, Koffo encountered unforeseen obstacles. Despite his best efforts to infiltrate Gilde Meister's computer system remotely, the virtual barriers proved insurmountable, thwarting his attempts at every turn.

Undeterred, Koffo and his team resolved to confront the challenge head-on, embarking on a daring mission to breach the company's defences from within. With hearts pounding with anticipation, they descended upon the Chief Engineer's office, their determination unwavering as they prepared to confront the final hurdle standing between them and their objective.

"Umm!" he gasped, shifting uncomfortably on his chair.

"Is everything okay?" asked Sabon-Gari.

"Ah…yes, just trying to enter the pass." Koffo replied, while simultaneously reaching out for his mirror. He recalled the password by uttering some magic words, as the others were anxiously watching. Sabon-Gari was robbing his hands in anticipation.

Koffo looked at the password intently and then carefully entered each alphabet, letter, and symbol into the computer with a finger and access was finally granted.

"Phew!" he heaved a sigh of relief as his serious look quickly gave way to a smile.

He carefully probed and combed through the computer system, sifting through files and folders looking for information and documents. After about twenty minutes and a couple of clicks and searches, the wizard had access to the data he was looking for. Koffo spent some time snooping and scanning through the thicket of statistics in the vast database as he burrowed deep into the system and rummaged around for useful information. "Yes, here it is! This is it!" he whispered. Excitedly, they all moved closer to the computer and stirred at the screen. "Now, we'll have to download everything… yes, everything!" said Koffo rubbing his hands in glee and then dipping his hand in his pocket, he produced two USB sticks.

After their successful operation at Gilde Meister, the Weafric2w team was again on the prowl. In similar fashions, they also carried out perfectly executed missions and succeeded at obtaining confidential information from the computers of two other companies – the slight risk also added zest to the experience.

At the end of their operations, they had in their possession USB sticks containing commercial secrets, blueprints, and other valuable information about the companies' products, as well as some of their mode of operation and surveillance data. The African wizards and the witch were filled with a sense of accomplishment and thought their finest hour had come.

"Wow!" Koffo exclaimed, punching the air triumphantly amid back-patting when they got back to their base. He did a little victory dance. "I've always wanted to do this! I've always known we could do it! Now, we have some of the master keys, yes, the golden keys to open some doors. Thank you, lady and gentlemen for a job well done! The prospects are incredible!" he enthused, brimming with joy and pride. Koffo found it hard to believe they had succeeded in their mission of secretly obtaining some of the industrial secrets of these big companies. They were in a celebration mood all through the night and Koffo decided to travel with the team back home.

Two days later, Uwe, one of the company's security experts, accidentally discovered the security breach of their computer system during a routine check. He reported his observation to Bernd, his assistant who in turn, informed Wolfgang, the Chief Executive Officer.

"I suspect our system has been broken into," said Bernd to Wolfgang.

"How could that be when we only recently upgraded our security system? I thought we took some steps the last time with some recommendation from Mr Klaus to upgrade and make our system more secure to protect our database and systems from nasty viruses and hackers?" asked the CEO, with a puzzled look on his face.

"Yes, sir, that is correct. And that's the more reason I'm surprised because the security software we recently acquired is among the best, the most modern, and trusted around for a secure VPN that encrypts data. Its main feature is helping to keep our private information private by masking our IP addresses" replied Bernd. "However, just a while ago, Uwe drew my attention to the signals of a breach in one of the trackers of our security apparatus," he added.

After checking the security devices of the database together, they found out that the tracking devices that showed the log where some of their sensitive data was stored had been breached. "The hackers must have had access to our database, the indicators show that," said Wolfgang, rather alarmed.

"They might have gained access into the volt where our interim sample gadgets and the sensitive information of our exclusive, yet-to-be-patented research and invention for our future designs are also stored," added the CEO, who was obsessive about secrecy and security.

"It still beats me how they gained access to our system," replied Bernd, running his hand over his hair. "And you know, sir, the issue of security is becoming very serious, and due to the increasing activities of criminal hackers, many establishments are beefing up their digital defences but, like I told you, everyday internet fraud is becoming more and more sophisticated; The truth is that as technology gets smarter, cybercriminals are becoming cleverer and complete security may not be possible because sometimes, given enough time and motivation, a determined adversary will always be able to penetrate a targeted system. Moreover, these modern Virtual Private Networks that we've got are the same protective networks other large companies and even many governments use to keep outsiders from accessing their information," added Bernd.

"And how 're you sure this is not the handiwork of our competitors?" asked Wolfgang.

"This I cannot answer exactly," replied Bernd.

"Bernd, you're well aware that we own one of Deutschland's proudest companies whose heritage and reputation is the pride of many, including our government," said Wolfgang. "We cannot afford to lose vital information which we have spent an enormous amount of time and resources over the years to develop; This is our foundation as well as our future," he added.

Subsequently, the CEO summoned Klaus, the Chief of Operations and Michael, the Computer Systems Analyst, to his office to discuss the issue.

⊷⊶⊰❖⊱⊷⊶

Chapter 6

Jenny, Where Are You?

The disappearance of Jenny cast a heavy shadow over Hexenburg, leaving the community reeling with shock and sorrow. As the days passed with no sign of her, the town's sense of unease deepened, exacerbated by the fruitless efforts of the police to locate her.

For Petra, the weight of uncertainty bore down heavily, her thoughts consumed by the fate of her missing daughter. Each passing moment brought fresh waves of anguish, her heart heavy with worry for Jenny's safety. Despite her turmoil, Petra found solace in the unwavering support of her husband, Dieter, whose steadfast presence provided a beacon of hope amidst the darkness.

Dieter, though grappling with his trauma, remained resolute in his determination to find Jenny. Taking a leave of absence from work, he dedicated himself fully to the search, tirelessly scouring every corner of Hexenburg in pursuit of any clue that might lead to his daughter's whereabouts.

Meanwhile, young Kai, usually so full of energy and mischief, became a sombre figure, his usual laughter replaced by a solemn silence as he grappled with the absence of his beloved sister.

During their grief, the community rallied around the distraught family, offering words of comfort and support in their time of need. Led by Fritz and Walter, two respected teachers from the Hexenburg School of Witches, a group of

Jenny's classmates and fellow pupils arrived at the family's home, each bearing a lantern lit with solemn reverence.

Gathered in the dim light of evening, the atmosphere was heavy with sorrow as they stood in solidarity with Petra and Dieter, offering their condolences and support in the face of such overwhelming loss. In that moment, surrounded by the flickering glow of lanterns, they found solace in their shared grief, united in their determination to hold onto hope in the face of adversity.

"We 're all concerned by what we're hearing and devastated by the news!" said Fritz, after Petra had ushered her guests in.

"Yes, my dear, this is the situation we've found ourselves!" answered Petra.

"This incident has broken the heart of our community and we're here to tell you that, no matter what, we shall find Jenny. Have you heard anything from the police?" asked Fritz.

"No, not yet, but the police have been working hard to find Jenny," answered Petra. "Besides interrogating her various friends to get any information that could give a clue of her whereabouts, they've also dispatched specialist teams and equipment and carrying out searches everywhere in our neighbourhood and the environs assisted by dogs, but there're still more questions than answers at this point in the police investigation," she added dolefully, still trying to come to terms with the disappearance of her daughter.

"Petra, don't worry, there'll be some good news!" said Walter reassuringly. We're taking the situation very seriously and are determined to get to the bottom of the matter. Jenny's such a nice and lovely girl and I can only imagine how you feel without your little girl being home for the past few days. I can't understand how she could have simply disappeared from the room just like that," continued Walter.

"Indeed, that is unheard of and very strange!" added Fritz.

"It's a mystery and we have no explanation; Her disappearance is out of character, and we're concerned about her well-being," said Dieter.

After their discussion concluded, the delegation prepared to depart, and Petra expressed her gratitude to them for their visit and support. Despite attempting to maintain a casual demeanour, her guests could see the worry etched on her face, prompting them to offer words of encouragement and strength.

Following the delegation's departure, Petra found herself unable to shake off her deep-seated concern for Jenny's well-being. Despite placing some faith in the efforts of the police, her anxiety gnawed at her, compelling her to take matters into her own hands.

Turning to her oracle once more in a desperate bid for answers, Petra placed her crystal ball on the table in her room. With a fervent plea and the invocation of ancient words, she hoped to unlock the mystery of her daughter's disappearance.

"Vom treffpunkt aus zwei parallelen linien. Ete, Beta - ich flehe auch an - Verzaubern!" she said the magic words. As she gazed into the swirling depths of the crystal ball, blurry images flickered across its surface, revealing glimpses of a shadowy figure confined in a dimly lit enclosure. Despite her efforts to focus and clarify the vision, the image remained elusive, slipping further from her grasp with each attempt.

Frustrated and deeply troubled by the unusual nature of the vision, Petra resolved to seek guidance from her boss, Ursula, hoping that together they might unravel the enigma that had gripped her heart with fear.

"I would like to meet you urgently to discuss something very important," said Petra on the telephone, as she removed her gaze from the iridescent crystal ball. And then, she went on to brief Ursula about her observation in her crystal ball.

"That's very strange!" replied the school director. "Okay, if 13:00 is convenient for you, then you may come to me at home so we can investigate the situation. I have an appointment with Karl at this time so he could be around, too," she added.

"That would be fine. See you then!" answered Petra.

Ursula, who had a bird comfortably perching on her shoulder, smilingly ushered her guests into her sitting room. After exchanging pleasantries, she quickly prepared them some coffee. Ursula could see that Petra wanted her to immediately get on with the issue that brought her there and the former soon got down to business.

Ursula went into her room and returned with her crystal ball which she carefully placed on the table. Stretching her hands towards the magic ball, the witch mouthed some magic words. A blurred image of Jenny, soon, appeared on the face of the crystal ball and they were not able to get the rolling pictures and the image of a girl that appeared to be holed up somewhere in focus, just like Petra had also observed.

Ursula turned off her divination apparatus and reached for her magic wand and with it, she gently struck the surface of the crystal ball three times and intoned, "Die hueter des dreizehnten welt, Eta, Beta - ich rufe auch an

- Verzaubern!"

At that moment, glowing strands of light flickered and moved across the inside surface of the ball and a high-resolution image of Jenny appeared on the surface of the ball. Ursula gently waved her wand over the surface of the crystal ball to plug her location and to retain the enhanced picture of the zoomed-in scene around Jenny.

And then, like scenes from a movie came revealing pictures running on the screen of the crystal ball. They were surprised to see a relatively miniature Jenny on a table surrounded by a group of Africans. It was uncanny and for the next ten minutes they sat transfixed as they peered at the clear pictures of the crystal ball in front of them in utter disbelief.

The leader of the African wizard team carefully lifted the tiny, remodelled Jenny from her miniature box, intending to offer her some nourishment. However, Jenny appeared bewildered and apprehensive in the presence of these towering figures who seemed to loom over her like colossal giants. With wide, fearful eyes, she surveyed her surroundings, struggling to comprehend the bizarre scenario unfolding before her.

Confusion clouded Jenny's thoughts as she grappled with her reduced size and the perplexing sight of the African wizards. She couldn't fathom how she had shrunk to such proportions or why these towering beings held her in their grasp. The surreal nature of the situation left her questioning whether she was caught during a vivid dream.

As Jenny pondered her predicament, memories flooded back to her mind in a rush. Recollections of a dream she had experienced before her journey to Africa now merged with her current reality, blurring the lines between the two. Fatigue weighed heavily on her as she rubbed her eyes, struggling to adjust to the dim light within the confines of her small enclosure, further adding to her disorientation.

"Helloo!" Sabon-Gari deep voice suddenly broke the silence in the room. It was an unfamiliar voice. Jenny looked up at the unfamiliar dark faces staring down at her - she didn't recognize any of them. "Who are you and why are you people holding me here?" asked Jenny after a while, feeling rather scared.

"Have no fear, my daughter, we're your friends. You're safe here," replied the African wizards' leader, genially. There was a deep and rich resonance to his voice.

"What's your name?" he asked.

Jenny looked up at his face and the faces of the others and cringed.

"I want to go home!" she said.

"Have no fear, my daughter. We'll take you home," replied Sabon-Gari calmly. "What is your name?" he asked.

"My name is Jenny," replied the pocket-sized Jenny after a brief pause and then she stood up on the table.

"You're a pretty girl, Jenny! Your mother is equally a beautiful woman. What's your mother called?" asked the leader with a slow, mysterious smile playing between his lips.

"My mother's name is Petra," answered Jenny.

"And your father?"

Jenny paused and, once again, scanned the faces peering down at her from all sides. Though Sabon-Gari sounded friendly, Jenny sensed he could be dangerous. The cryptic, treacherous gleam in the leader's eyes and the sly and penetrating gaze of the others made her feel uncomfortable.

"You're an absolute diamond ... very soon, you'll be back home," said Sabon-Gari reassuringly. "Tell me, what is the name of your father?"

"Dieter…Dieter Engelberg," replied Jenny, staring straight at him.

"Jenny, you must be tired, now, go in and have a rest." said the leader, who then ordered her some food, after she had walked gingerly back to her cage.

The two Hexenburg witches and the wizard were horrified after watching the revelation from the crystal ball.

"Oh no, they've transformed Jenny!" she cried.

"Looks like we have a serious case on our hands. They could be predatory elements who visited you and abducted Jenny," said Ursula.

"But why Jenny? What has she done? What do they want from her?" asked Petra with an apprehensive look on her face and her panicked mind grappled for answers.

"Answering these questions at this moment is like deconstructing a puzzle of fiendish complexity," replied Karl-Heinz. "If we don't know what's going on, we can't make any informed decision and for now we can only theorize about their possible motives." he added.

"Indeed, my dear, there're benevolent and malevolent witches, but first, we need to know exactly what is happening here." Added Ursula, placing her hand on Petra's shoulder to console her.

"But what ominous spider had woven their web around my daughter and looking to infest us with their poison?" Cried Petra.

The Hexenburg team suspected they were contending with malevolent forces, prompting Ursula, Petra, and Karl-Heinz to delve deeper into the unfolding mystery. With a determined resolve, Ursula summoned Jenny's image once more, her hand delicately tracing over the surface of the crystal ball to rewind the scenes and uncover the origin of the African wizards' clandestine activities. As they peered intently into the shimmering depths of the magic ball, they observed the meticulously orchestrated manoeuvres of the African wizards.

In the ethereal glow of the crystal ball, the trio witnessed the organized departure of the African wizards from their base, soaring through the night sky on palm fronds until they reached Jenny's residence under the cover of darkness. Seizing Jenny from her slumber, the wizards swiftly whisked her away, returning to their base hidden within the confines of the Westfalen Park.

As Ursula traced the path of the African wizards back to the park, Karl-Heinz recognized the distinctive silhouette of the television tower looming in the background—a prominent landmark of Dortmund's Westfalen Park. A sombre silence descended upon the room as the gravity of their discovery settled upon them, leaving them perturbed by the realization of the supernatural forces at play.

Petra's heart sank as she grappled with the sense of failure as a witch to safeguard her daughter from harm. Overwhelmed by a wave of apprehension and sorrow, she was moved to tears at the sight of her daughter ensnared in a perilous situation, her safety now hanging precariously in the balance.

Determined to uncover the truth, the trio intensified their efforts to gather intelligence on their mysterious adversaries, closely monitoring their movements and activities through the arcane insights of their crystal balls. With each passing moment, they conducted discreet investigations, piecing together fragments of information to unravel the enigmatic operations of the African wizards.

As the day unfolded, the Hexenburg team meticulously pieced together the puzzle, scrutinizing the intricate web of events involving the African wizards. Through the revelations of their magic ball, Ursula, Petra, and Karl-Heinz were confronted with the shocking truth of the wizards' covert infiltration into various firms to pilfer industrial secrets—a revelation that left them reeling in disbelief and apprehension.

"I think something pretty dire has been happening; Right away, we'll be going to the Park on a reconnaissance mission!" said Ursula to her colleagues.

"This could be the tip of the iceberg! It could be a network!" Replied Karl-Heinz.

"I wonder how long they've been living and operating here?" said Petra.

The African witches and wizards' reputation in dealing with their victims was known to her, and that was the source of her mild anxiety. At the same time, she had spent more than a week in Africa and as a witch herself, she tried to find out first-hand more about African witchcraft during her visit to the continent. She had read some books as well as heard various stories about the naked cruelty of the African witches and wizards.

"African witches have a history," said Petra. And then she went further, "They are very wicked, and their craft and every move are all about destruction, that is how they are. They have ruined the lives of many, and the theatre of death and disaster is never far away from them."

"Who knows, there could be a correlation between your trip to Africa and Jenny's abduction," noted Karl-Heinz.

"I suppose it's remotely possible," replied Petra, as the truth suddenly began to dawn on her, and it disturbed her to realize this might be the case. "But shouldn't we inform the police?" she asked.

"Oh, no, no, not yet!" replied Ursula. "For now, we 're just beginning to see the individual trees, but we cannot understand the forest - I'd like us to dig a bit deeper to know more about the exact location of these mysterious people," she added.

Ursula felt such a case required a subtle approach. She also felt the police could do little in such paranormal cases as they might not totally understand it.

"We don't have much information about these people and there is a bit of murkiness in terms of how they operate," said Karl-Heinz, stroking his beard. Karl-Heinz was a man of few words. He had fire burning inside him but, on the surface, he was like an ice pack of ice.

With a sudden burst of insight, the Hexenburg team found themselves face to face with the gravity of their situation. They understood the urgency of rescuing Jenny and reclaiming the stolen data, yet the prospect of involving the authorities seemed fraught with uncertainty. Nevertheless, they resolved to maintain strict surveillance over the African wizards from that moment onward.

Driven by their determination, Ursula, Petra, and Karl-Heinz embarked on a covert mission to the Westfalen Park in Dortmund. As they navigated through the park, their keen eyes took in every detail—the huts, the cottage, the layout of the surroundings. Despite the urgency of the situation, they refrained from immediate action, recognizing the need for careful deliberation.

Returning to Hexenburg, Ursula and Karl-Heinz convened to weigh their options and strategize their next moves, while Petra remained behind at the park to maintain a physical presence and monitor developments first-hand. Fully cognizant of the challenges ahead, they understood that confronting the African wizards would require meticulous planning and considerable resources.

"We must also consider bolstering our ranks, particularly in securing control over the airspace above

Westfalen Park to prevent the wizards from escaping," Ursula emphasized, acknowledging the need for numerical strength and aerial dominance.

After thorough deliberation and careful consideration of their resources, Ursula and Karl-Heinz made a pivotal decision. They opted to enlist the support of Hexenburg's finest students, selecting a diverse group of twelve individuals from different classes to form a specialized team tasked with the mission to rescue Jenny.

"We've got something on our hands," the school director announced to the team of young witches and wizards who assembled in a class the next day. Walter and Fritz, two of the most senior teachers in the school, but who were not part of the team, were also present.

"We've now uncovered the secret and some of the damnable activities of some African wizards who have kidnapped Jenny and held her captive in Dortmund." began Ursula. "Not only that, in Dortmund, there are extraordinary things happening. Let me show you what we're dealing with, right now." she continued, as she reached for her crystal ball and placed it on the table in front of the class.

And then pointing her magic wand at the magic ball, the director chanted some magic words and Jenny's pictures appeared on the face of the magic ball. Ursula, subsequently, touched and scrolled the face of the oracle, like one changing the pictures on a touch screen gadget, and the team watched scene after scene of the secret activities of the African wizards and the young Hexenburg witches and wizards were shocked by the unsettling images they had seen in the crystal ball.

"But why have they kidnapped Jenny? What do they want from her?" asked Christa, a member of the team.

"That's one element that's a mystery we must solve," replied Ursula.

"Darm, these people constitute a danger to everybody!" said Martin.

"Yes, they pose a very potential threat; And there's another more sinister possibility of them committing more crimes and we must do something to stop them quickly." added Fritz.

"Yes, I think we have to urgently move to take care of these wicked people before they take care of us." cut in Walter.

"These people pose a threat that cannot be ignored. It has never happened that foreign witches or wizards came to our territory, our backyard, to overpower us. We're the Hexenburg witches and wizards, well known for our craft. We'll not allow this to happen and certainly not in my time!" declared Ursula, with a stern look on her face. Karl-Heinz could not recall when she last saw the school director looking so grim. He nodded in agreement and added, "Now, we'll have to work things out to meet the challenges of these dark forces on our soil."

"I think we should visit them on the sly and take them by surprise to free Jenny," offered Martin. Ursula nodded approvingly. The school director was struck by Martin's thoughtfulness and sensitivity to what they had in front of them. He was an intelligent, inter-active and curious young man, and he seemed to be ahead of his peers.

The other members of the team put forward various ideas on how they thought their African adversaries could be shackled. They also discussed steps to shield themselves against any attack by the African wizards and the team drew up a 'plan B' in case of any unforeseen problems.

Subsequently, Ursula unfolded their final plans to the team, plans aimed at setting Jenny free. The members of the Hexenburg team would be strategically positioned to try to seal off the park's air space, while Ursula and Karl-Heinz would go in to meet the Africans to secure Jenny's release.

"We have to prepare for every possibility against these predators." said Ursula.

The Hexenburg team finalized their plans to infiltrate Westfalen Park within two days, opting to maintain constant surveillance on the African wizards until then. With their strategies in place, the team ventured into an open field to hone their aerial combat skills in preparation for the upcoming mission. Excitement and determination filled the air as the young Hexenburg witches and wizards showcased their prowess with youthful vigour. Martin executed a flawless double somersault before striking a human-sized figure suspended from a high platform, while Erwin demonstrated expert precision with a reverse manoeuvre, hitting a figure suspended from a tree branch.

Meanwhile, a group of six wizards executed intricate aerial formations, captivating the attention of onlookers, including Karl-Heinz. Following intensive planning and training exercises, the team eagerly anticipated their mission in Dortmund the next day.

As preparations were going on, Ursula dispatched one of her birds to deliver a message to Lahm, a respected wizard and close friend of her late father residing in Osnabruck. She sought to update him on recent developments and inform him of the potential need for his assistance soon.

"Hello, Twinkle, nice to see you, my friend! How are you doing, today?" Joachim, Lahm's amiable son, addressed the bird as soon as it arrived and perched on one of the dead tree trunks that was lying on the ground beside the house where they lived. The youngster was fond of the bird and often played with it whenever the family visited Ursula.

Before long, Lahm noticed the scroll nestled within a small, light transparent plastic container tethered to one of the bird's wings. "Ah, there, you've brought something for me!" he exclaimed, mirroring his father's familiar gait as he approached the bird with his feet facing backwards. With practiced ease, he carefully untied the container from the bird's leg and made his way to deliver the message to his father, who was reclining on a sofa with his feet contorted in an unusual manner. Both father and son possessed the rare ability to rotate their feet in the opposite direction and walk effortlessly in this unconventional stance.

Lahm opened the little plastic container and brought out a little piece of paper. In it was the message:

"One of our own has been bound by the malignant spell of some remote adversaries and intruders. May need your help, soon! With love!"

Later that afternoon, right after the mesmerizing air show, Denis, a key member of the rescue mission team, crossed paths with his friends Damian and Daniel as they were heading home. Damian, affectionately dubbed 'Bully Boy' by his peers, was known for his confrontational and fiery demeanour, often exhibiting traits of dominance and aggression. His tendency to bully others had been a cause of concern for the school authorities. However, beneath his tough exterior, Damian harboured a vulnerable side, still grappling with the complexities of adolescence.

"The air display today was fantastic," said Damian. "What is it all about?" he asked.

"It was just a training session to rescue Jenny who has been kidnapped by a group of Africans in Dortmund." answered Denis. "But it is still a secret; Do not tell anybody about this just yet," he added.

"African wizards? So, they kidnapped Jenny who had been declared missing for the past few days?" said Damian. "Crazy stuff! So, have they informed the police yet?" he asked.

"No, not yet. For some reasons, Mrs. Ursula has decided not to involve the police." replied Denis. "You see, we're still very much in the dark about this and nobody knows what's going on, but we 're sure they have Jenny." he added.

"Uhm, I see... that's very interesting!" said Damian. "But you don't need a team of one thousand people to carry out a simple rescue operation. All that is required is to develop the right approach, the right tactics, and strategies, you and I can do that." said Damian sublimely.

"Trust you to say a crazy thing like that!" cut in Daniel, who had hitherto been listening with rapt attention to his friends' conversation. "But you have no idea the kind of people you're dealing with at the other end." Daniel added.

"Damian, you must be very crazy to conceive of the idea of us going to take on those wicked and dangerous African wizards who live in thatched huts in the Dortmund Westfalen Park. You haven't even seen them yet! They look really mean from what I saw in the crystal ball and not the ones to fool around with," added Denis.

"Did you say wicked and dangerous?' asked Damian. "Now, tell me, who could be more dangerous than us? Have you forgotten how we used to eliminate those stubborn and more dangerous monsters and aliens?" continued Damian, whose expertise at killing virtual monsters and aliens from space and other realms in special computer programmes was well-known to his friends.

"Ha ha ha... computer games! That is just in the computer. But we're discussing real life here!" Denis sneered.

"Denis, I know that sometimes you talk like a little girl. These African wizards are not different. We can work out a good strategy to clip their wings and set Jenny free and become real life heroes in the process," declared Damian. "you people seem to have forgotten who we are, we're the Hexenburg wizards, the greatest in Deutschland and everybody knows that. You don't have to be frightened. All I want to hear now is that both of you are ready to team up with me to free Jenny." said Damian.

"Tell me, when is your proposed mission to Dortmund taking place?" he asked.

"Tomorrow." Answered Denis.

"Alright, and what time did the team proposed to be there?" Inquired Damian.

"In the afternoon." Replied Denis.

"Okay," said Damian. "let's plan our strategy and get all we need, right away; Then, very early tomorrow morning before the other team gets there, we'd already be in Dortmund to set Jenny free and surprise them." added Damian confidently.

"So, what strategies have you got to set Jenny free?" asked Daniel raising his eyebrow and looking askance at Damian.

"Good question!" answered Damian. "Now, listen. We'll need the invisible cream so that they cannot see us; Once we're able to track them down with the aid of our crystal ball, we'll then take them unaware, caging and putting them under our control using our invisible nets. After getting them under wraps and setting Jenny free, we can then contact Mrs. Ursula and the three of us will be the real heroes." declared Damian.

"Well, your plan doesn't sound bad in theory." remarked Daniel, after a brief pause.

"Look friends, we can do it and become heroes," enthused Damian. And he went further, "now we need a good name for our team. How about calling our team ... uhm ... D3?" asked Damian. That stands for Damian, Denis, and Daniel,' he added.

"That sounds good, but I think 3D would be a better name," said Daniel.

"Yes, 3D sounds better. I like it!" replied Damian. "We're assuming the name 3D. Denis, what do you think?" asked Damian.

"Uhm ... I don't know. Though I like the idea, I still have my doubts," replied Denis.

"Denis, you must be a real man. You see, with our powers, we can take care of these African wizards and achieve something momentous by freeing Jenny." said Damian. "Now, let's go quickly to get all the things we need," he added confidently.

Reluctantly, Denis agreed to join Damian and Daniel in their endeavour to free Jenny. Damian's assurance that they could become heroes if successful provided a significant boost to their confidence.

Meanwhile, in Westfalen Park, Petra, who had been diligently monitoring the situation, learned that the Wafric2w team planned to depart the following day, likely after midnight. With this crucial information, she deemed it safe to return to Hexenburg that evening to strategize with her colleagues.

With all the pieces of the puzzle now in place, the African wizards prepared to return home. Sabon-Gari instructed Koffo to inform the team about a planned gathering for some leisure time in the park before their departure the next day.

Upon receiving the message, Mulumba went to Boniface's hut to relay the news, only to find it empty.

Knowing his friend's habits, Mulumba suspected Boniface might be sleeping as a bird in a nearby tree hollow close to the baker's cottage. Transforming into a cat, Mulumba set out to locate his friend.

"Boniface! Bon... ni...face!" the cat called out from below the foot of the tree. A bird suddenly emerged from a hollow in the tree and sat on the trunk.

"Ah-ah, Mulumba, what is it? Why won't you let me relax in peace? Can't you see it's still very early!" said the bird.

"Good morning, my feathered friend. I'm sorry to disturb you, can you spare me a minute?" asked the cat.

"But how long will I keep telling you if you wake up early, that you shouldn't disturb everyone else?" asked the bird.

"But it's already morning, my dear, can't you hear the calls of the birds?" replied the cat and then added, "Now, listen carefully and you'll hear the birds singing out there.'

Just then, the bird suddenly flew back into the hollow in the tree.

"Boniface! Koboko!" the Cat called out.

The bird reappeared and perched on the edge of the hollowed-out trunk of the tree.

"Listen Mulumba, if you've got anything important to tell me then, for goodness's sake, allow me some rest." pleaded the bird.

"I only wanted to let you know that Koffo has invited us to his house to eat some African food with bush meat." said the Cat.

As soon as the bird heard African food and bush meat, it exclaimed, "Oh!' and suddenly, flew off from the tree trunk where it perched to join its friend on the ground and suddenly transformed into a man from its bird form.

"You should have said so right away, instead of beating around the bush," replied Boniface. "So, your Royal Majesty, when is the eating show happening?" he asked smilingly. The cat transformed back into a human form. "Around noon," replied Mulumba, as they both headed off to meet their colleagues.

Later in the day, after a visit to Koffo in the city centre, the Weafric2w team returned to Westfalen Park. They found a shady spot under a low tree and relaxed for a while, enjoying the peaceful surroundings. Eventually, they decided to take a leisurely walk around the park, soaking in the beauty of their surroundings. They wandered along the park's waterways, appreciating the serene atmosphere and the stunning scenery.

Afterwards, they indulged in some friendly canoe games in one of the park's small pools. With their missions completed, the African wizards and the witch looked forward to returning home the next day, feeling satisfied with their accomplishments.

Chapter 7

The Confrontation

On the sixth day since Jenny's abduction, the atmosphere in Westfalen Park seemed serene and unassuming. Mulumba, an early riser, greeted the day with a sense of optimism. With the sun barely peeking over the horizon, he made his way to Boniface's hut, anticipating their usual morning chat. He had heard Boniface's distinctive howl, a signal of his friend's wakefulness.

Entering the hut, Mulumba found Boniface already awake, his demeanour reflecting a similar eagerness for their impending journey back home. The two friends settled in, ready to unwind and engage in their customary discussions. As they sipped on their morning brew, they exchanged anecdotes and reflections on their experiences during their first-ever trip to Europe. Each shared their impressions of the unfamiliar sights and sounds they had encountered, adding a touch of excitement to the conversation.

"Wow, mission accomplished! Who could have dreamt it? And, to add icing to the cake, we have the industrial secrets, too," said Mulumba with a big smile on his face.

"My brother, what a time to be alive! The future suddenly looks so interesting and full of promise!" Answered Boniface smilingly, while simultaneously dusting the piece of tree trunk that served as a chair for his friend to sit down. "I spoke with Koffo yesterday, and it looks like the secrets we have in our possession are an incredible opportunity that could alter our lives forever, and soon, we are going to become Chief Executives!" he continued, his face swelled with hope and pride.

"So, Boniface, what are your immediate plans when we get back home?" asked Mulumba.

"Uhm…I haven't really thought about it; Maybe I'll go into some business or something in that line," answered Boniface, a smile lighting up his face.

"Well as for me, depending on how things flow, first, I 'm going to surprise Stella." said Mulumba.

"You mean, Stella, your girlfriend?" asked Boniface.

"Yes," replied Mulumba, looking away and staring at the thatched roof of the hut. "You know, Stella told me I'm a failure, and that I can never be rich in my life!" he added.

"You mean, Stella told you that?" asked Boniface.

"Yes, she did!" replied Mulumba.

"I thought Stella was such a nice and quiet lady." Boniface remarked.

"Ha, Stella? Quiet? That lady's nothing but a slow poison!" said Mulumba.

While Mulumba and Boniface engaged in their morning conversation, Damian, Denis, and Daniel embarked on their journey to Westfalen Park, unaware of the significant events unfolding around them. It was a twist of fate that brought them to the park on the very day Sabon-Gari and his team were preparing to depart for their homeland.

Meanwhile, Petra, the school director, received a call that morning, instructing her to return home and coordinate efforts with other colleagues in Dortmund and neighbouring towns. They had been alerted to the presence of the African wizards and witches and were conducting discreet surveillance using their crystal balls, monitoring both the Africans and the surrounding airspace.

As Damian, Denis, and Daniel approached the park, they tread cautiously through the tranquil surroundings, the only sounds accompanying them being the chirping of birds. Crossing a small wooden bridge devoid of water, they made their way toward the clustered huts nestled closely together. Damian, ever vigilant, crept toward the nearest hut, peering cautiously through a narrow opening to check for any signs of occupancy. Whispering to his companions that it was empty, he proceeded to inspect the next hut similarly. With each hut revealing no occupants, Denis quietly circled to the third hut, keeping a watchful eye for any surprises.

"They're in here!" he whispered to the others.

Damian and Daniel, soon, joined him. Damian's beady eyes swept around the little room of the hut.

"But I can't see Jenny in there," said Damian in a low tone to his companions, after watching the unsuspecting African wizards in the hut for a while.

Then, the Hexenburg wizards magically opened one of their invisible nets and quickly spread it on the ground behind the hut. Damian recited some special words and suddenly, the thin film of the invisible net rose from the ground and spread over the hut's complete exterior. The two Weafric wizards were caged!

Damian punched the air in triumph. 'We've got them! Wow, we've got the African wizards!' he said. The three youngsters were beside themselves with excitement. Denis promptly telephoned Ursula who was sitting in her office to surprise her with the cheering news.

"We've caught the African wizards! Damian, Daniel, and I have them, right now, in our net!" said Denis triumphantly over the phone.

"Really? You have the African wizards?" asked Ursula, somewhat taken aback to hear the news.

"Yes, we have them; Come quickly to the Westfalen park in Dortmund!" replied Denis.

"Tell me, how many of them do you have?" she asked.

"We've got two of them in our net!" answered Denis proudly.

"But there're more of them there!" said Ursula, a little bit alarmed that the youngsters could be in danger. "Look, I want you to hang on there and do nothing else... I'll be with you right away!" she added.

After her discussion with Denis, Ursula wasted no time in contacting Karl-Heinz to relay the latest developments. "The situation with the people holding Jenny is precarious. It's like walking on a razor's edge; mishandling it could spell disaster," Ursula cautioned urgently. "Please, head straight to Westfalen Park without delay to intercept those youngsters before things escalate. I'll gather my belongings and join you shortly. Time is of the essence!"

Just as Ursula finished her call, Brigitte, the team leader who had been closely monitoring the situation, rang in with an update. Armed with this new information, Ursula swiftly mobilized her team, rallying them to action. The news of the young Hexenburg wizards' successful capture of the African wizards filled them with a mix of surprise and determination. With a sense of urgency, they hurried to gather the necessary equipment from their storage rooms, their anticipation mounting as they prepared to spring into action.

Meanwhile, in a twist of fate, Sabon-Gari, adorned with his signature dark glasses, was en route to meet Toyosi when he felt compelled to check on the others. Arriving at the scene, he approached the huts cautiously, his senses tingling with a sense of impending danger. As he neared one of the huts, he noticed a faint outline of a net encircling it, invisible yet discernible to his trained eye. His curiosity piqued, Sabon-Gari circled the hut, only to come face to face with the trio of Hexenburg wizards who had already spotted him.

"Uh-oh!" Daniel gasped timidly as his heart skipped.

Denis gave a nervous chuckle and was trying to remain composed, but he could feel a fluttering pulse deep down, apprehensive that something unpleasant might happen.

Sabon-Gari would naturally detest any bid to cage him or any of his colleagues and when he discovered this, he felt he'd to do what was expedient to free them and he edged towards the three youngsters and accosted them.

"What have you done? Set them free!" the bespectacled leader said gruffly, with a stern look on his face.

"Where's Jenny? Where's Jenny?" replied Damian, rather undaunted.

"I say, set them free, immediately!" the grim-faced leader thundered and scowled at Damian with a cold malevolent look in his face and his voice harsh and penetrating, while simultaneously taking off his glasses.

"Where's Jenny? Where did you hide her?" Damian yelled out at the leader.

"Jenny! Jenny! Are you there?" Denis and Daniel called out looking inside the hut from the closed door.

As the commotion outside intensified, Mulumba and Boniface frantically attempted to break free from their confinement. However, the invisible, elastic magical net had ensnared the hut completely, rendering their efforts futile. Their attempts to open the door proved fruitless, leaving them trapped inside.

Outside, tensions escalated as Sabon-Gari and Damian engaged in a heated confrontation. With a swift gesture,

Sabon-Gari wielded his walking stick, and chanted, "Chaubun-nagun-gamugg!" – The wand unleashed a torrent of concentrated heat towards Damian, knocking him off balance.

Undeterred, Damian quickly regained his footing, picked up his magic wand and defiantly directed it towards Sabon-Gari with a determined incantation, he retaliated, "Vom treffpunkt aus zwei parallelen linien. Eta, Beta, ich flehe auch - Verzaubern!" Damian chanted, unleashing a scorching wave of energy aimed at Sabon-Gari, narrowly missing its mark.

Refusing to yield, Sabon-Gari countered with his own spell, directing a barrage of flickering light strands towards Damian. Simultaneously, Damian launched another assault of electrically charged energy from his wand, resulting in a clash of opposing forces that crackled in the air like lightning.

Witnessing the struggle, Denis and Daniel sprang into action, combining their powers to bolster Damian's efforts. Together, they unleashed a powerful surge of electric energy that overwhelmed Sabon-Gari, causing him to stagger backward.

Enraged by their defiance, Sabon-Gari abruptly broke off from the confrontation, his patience wearing thin. With swift, fluid movements, he seemed to glide across the ground, closing in on Damian with deadly intent. Suddenly, his walking stick transformed into a serpent, striking Damian's hand with venomous precision. The searing pain elicited a piercing cry from Damian, prompting Denis to panic, unsure of how to respond to the sudden escalation of violence.

It was a desperate situation for Sabon-Gari and given the circumstances, he felt he had to act fast to rescue his colleagues. Then the leader proceeded quickly to set his caged colleagues free. But, tried as he might using his magic wand, he could not break the magic net, and neither could he create an opening in it.

By now, the youngsters were generating so much noise and Sabon-Gari didn't quite like that; Having a crowd was the last thing he wanted and, finally abandoning his attempt to rescue his colleagues, he moved briskly away from the scene.

Denis and Daniel, who rushed to Damian's assistance were both bemused by the development not knowing how best to respond to the situation. Daniel shouted for help and one of the park's employees who was working nearby ran to the scene.

"What happened?" inquired Jurgen,

"He was bitten by a snake!" replied Daniel, pointing at Damian who was grimacing pain.

"Bitten by a snake? What snake? <u>There're no</u> snakes here in the park." said the middle-aged man, named Jurgen, rather surprised.

"No, he was bitten by the wicked African wizard's walking stick ... please, help him quickly, he's going die!" said Denis.

"Uhm...bitten by a wizard's walking stick?' Jurgen asked, simultaneously looking at the double teeth marks of the snake bite on Damian's right hand. Everything looked strange to him. "We don't have snake venom antidote here. Hurry, call the paramedics!" shouted Jurgen, who immediately called the curator of the park on the phone before proceeding to administer first aid to Damian by quickly sucking out the venom from the double teeth marks around the bite through the wound site with his mouth.

Luckily, for Damian, Sabon-Gari didn't use the deadliest of his snakes and the venom from this one wasn't as strong as the bite from the others, but he would however need quick medical attention before the tiny molecules of the slow-killing neurotoxic venom got absorbed into his bloodstream which could shut down his body's nervous and respiratory systems in a matter of hours leading to asphyxiation.

In the meantime, Ursula was in a tearing hurry as she rushed home to pick up her tools before heading to Westfalen Park. And although Denis had called to give her some piece of positive news, however, deep down, the witch had a foreboding feeling that something could go wrong. Just then, her phone rang and as if to confirm her fears, a distraught Denis called again to inform her of the snake bite and the danger Damian was in. Ursula became extremely apprehensive upon hearing the news.

"Is this a joke or what?" she queried. "Okay, I'll be there in a short while!" she said, and subsequently gave the young wizard some instructions on how he could provide Damian with some first aid. The witch told him to use the power of his magic wand on the site of the snake bite to cushion the effect before the venom could spread to other parts of his body.

The school director sensed there could be real trouble and she was filled with apprehension. She was also increasingly concerned about Jenny's safety and so many thoughts whirled around her mind. She knew she had to get to park as quickly as possible.

"These kids are driving me to distraction today! What do they think we're doing? Why have they decided to take matters into their own hands? Do they think this is a child's play?" she murmured, as she hurried into her inner room. The witch emerged with her magic carpet which she spread out on the floor; Soon, it rose and was undulating in mid-air it waited for her to get on board. She carried a little box containing a sword, took her magic wand and was soon on her way to the Westfalen Park in Dortmund where trouble was brewing.

Meanwhile, after the attack on Damian and his unsuccessful attempt to set his colleagues free, all Sabon-Gari cared about was getting out of the park as quickly as possible. On his way, while hot footing it back to his cottage, he telephoned Malaika and Toyosi who had incidentally gone to see the witch that morning in her tree hut where she was nestled telling them to quickly get their things and wait for him at the secret location where their boat was parked. When he got to his cottage, the leader carefully placed the little wooden box housing Jenny, as well as the USB sticks containing the industrial secrets in a bag. He then collected his personal effects and hurried out to join the others.

There was a great deal of anxiety in the air when Karl-Heinz arrived at the park, followed by the Hexenburg team who came moments afterwards. Fortunately, Damian was feeling better after the administration of first aid on him by Jurgen, the park worker.

Fortunately for Damian, Sabon-Gari's snake attack wasn't the deadliest in his arsenal, and the venom injected was relatively mild compared to the more potent varieties. However, swift medical attention was imperative to prevent the slow-acting neurotoxic venom from causing catastrophic damage. The venom had the potential to infiltrate Damian's bloodstream, gradually shutting down his nervous and respiratory systems, and ultimately leading to asphyxiation. Time was of the essence to counteract its effects.

Meanwhile, Ursula hurriedly made her way home to gather her tools before rushing to Westfalen Park. Despite Denis' attempt to convey positive news, Ursula couldn't shake off a foreboding sense of dread. Her fears were confirmed when Denis called again, distraught over

Damian's snake bite and the ensuing danger he faced. Ursula's apprehension mounted upon receiving the news. "Is this a joke or what?" she queried. "Okay, I'll be there in a short while!" She replied.

Quickly composing herself, Ursula instructed Denis on administering first aid to Damian, advising him to utilize the power of his magic wand to mitigate the effects of the venom at the site of the snake bite. "These kids are driving me to distraction today! What do they think we're doing? Why have they decided to take matters into their own hands? Do they think this is a child's play?" she murmured, as she hurried into her inner room. The witch emerged with her magic carpet which she spread out and suspended in the air above the floor, it was undulating in mid-air as it waited for her to get on board. With a sense of urgency, Ursula carried a little box containing a sword and took her magic wand and was soon on her way to Westfalen Park, her mind consumed with concern for Jenny's safety and the escalating situation at hand.

Meanwhile, Sabon-Gari, intent on leaving the park swiftly, contacted Malaika and Toyosi, instructing them to gather their belongings and rendezvous at the secret location where their boat was docked. After securing Jenny and the stolen USB sticks, Sabon-Gari hastily packed his personal effects and joined the others, eager to vacate the premises.

As tensions mounted, Karl-Heinz arrived at the park, followed closely by the Hexenburg team. Fortunately, Damian's condition had improved after receiving first aid from Jurgen, a park worker. Despite the palpable anxiety in the air, there was a glimmer of relief as Damian showed signs of recovery, providing a beacon of hope amidst the turmoil.

"What have you done? You guys have taken a great risk, and a lot of things could go wrong!" said Karl-Heinz, as he went close to assist the injured.

There was still an air of mystery surrounding these Africans and little was known about who they were or their mission in Germany and he was, therefore, surprised that the youngsters dared to unilaterally take on these foreign wizards.

"This will do you some good," said Karl-Heinz, as he applied the magic from his wand to Damian's wound. The young wizard could feel the soothing effect of the gentle radiation from the wand. Not long after, the paramedics arrived to take care of him. Now of immediate concern was Jenny's freedom.

"Who knows, the other African wizards might have left the park," said Karl-Heinz.

"No, they're still here," said Brigitte, the head of the surveillance team.

Karl-Heinz then asked Denis, Daniel and four others to stand guard over the captured African wizards while asking the other members of the Hexenburg team to go in search of the others. The youngsters were galvanized into action and were soon flying and searching all around the park for the other African wizards and the witch.

In the meantime, Sabon-Gari and his remaining colleagues had met at the secret location close to where their boat was concealed and were concurrently preparing to take off.

"So, what happened?" asked Malaika.

"They know we're here. It's no longer secure for us here in the park," replied Sabon-Gari. "For now, we're urgently switching locations, to return tonight and embark on our journey back home." added the leader.

"And, where're Mulumba and Boniface?" asked Toyosi.

"Looks like they're having some problems, but we'll see about them." replied the leader.

"And where're we heading?" inquired Toyosi, stirring at the leader aghast.

"Anywhere outside this park where nobody would recognize us," answered Sabon-Gari, as the feeling of unease swept through them for the first time.

Thereafter, the three covertly made a quick exit from their hideout in the park and took to the air. Unfortunately for the fleeing wizards and the witch, eagle-eyed Sabina spotted them in the distance. "There they are! They're getting away!" she alerted the other members of her team.

The Hexenburg witches and wizards swiftly pursued the fleeing Africans, unleashing a barrage of heat missiles and flickering light from their magic wands. Sabon-Gari retaliated, firing spells from his wand as they desperately attempted to escape the relentless assault. Outnumbered and outmanoeuvred, the African team found themselves overwhelmed, with no clear solution to counter the relentless onslaught from their adversaries.

As the chase intensified, Sabon-Gari's attention was suddenly drawn to the looming wind turbines ahead, their massive blades rotating ominously in the industrial landscape of Dortmund. Realizing the danger posed by the turbines, Sabon-Gari made a split-second decision to protect his remaining team members. With the Hexenburg witches closing in, he swiftly ordered Toyosi and Malaika to land, seeking refuge on the ground.

However, as the Africans began their descent, Martin, leading the charge for the Hexenburg team, launched a ferocious attack from his magic wand, targeting Toyosi with a stream of brilliant light. Struck on the leg, Toyosi plummeted from the sky, crashing into the grounds of a nearby IKEA warehouse. Sabon-Gari and Malaika rushed to his aid, helping him back to his feet as he grappled with a sharp pain in his knee from the fall.

Regrouping hastily, the Africans sought refuge within the confines of the warehouse, darting through the open main entrance with the Hexenburg team hot on their heels. The chase had reached a critical juncture, with the fate of both parties hanging in the balance amidst the intense pursuit.

Chapter 8

The Showdown

The morning dawned peacefully, just another Thursday at first glance. Yet, the day held pivotal significance for both the African team of wizards and the witch, desperate to secure Jenny's aid for their ailing leader, and the Hexenburg team, resolute in their mission to rescue Jenny from the clutches of their unwelcome visitors.

Leading the charge, Martin surged ahead, tracking the Africans into the warehouse. As he closed in on them, he confronted Sabon-Gari face to face, determined to thwart their escape. A brief scuffle ensued as Martin stood firm against the Weafric2w leader, blocking their path up the staircase.

In a sudden turn, Sabon-Gari landed a swift punch, catching Martin off guard and sending him to the ground. Undeterred, Martin rose to his feet, engaging in a fierce battle with the leader, delivering several rattling blows in the process. Amidst the chaos, Sabon-Gari's bag slipped from his grasp, landing tantalizingly close to Toyosi, who stood nearby, eyeing it intently.

With a swift incantation, Toyosi reached out, his hand extended towards the fallen bag. In a remarkable display of magic, the bag lifted from the ground, drawn towards him as if by an invisible force. Seconds before the approaching Hexenburg team could intercept, Toyosi seized the bag, casting a reassuring glance towards his master, indicating that all was well.

As tensions escalated and the Hexenburg team closed in, Toyosi and Malaika swiftly assessed the situation, darting off in opposite directions. The Hexenburg team pursued them relentlessly, their determination matching that of a pack of predators chasing their prey.

In her frantic bid to evade capture, Malaika ascended a staircase to the second floor, seeking refuge in an office. In her haste to flee, she inadvertently triggered an alarm by opening an emergency door. At that moment, Mirko and his Hexenburg team members, Andre, and Julia, burst into the office, ready to confront the fleeing intruder.

"What's happening?" asked one of the members of staff, who was sitting at her desk and looking rather surprised to see strangely attired teenagers crashing into her office.

"There, that woman!" replied Andre, pointing at the African. "We 're here to get her!" he added.

"You can't get away!" shouted Julia, as the three closed in on their adversary.

Realizing there was no way of getting away from her pursuers, Malaika decided to take up a fight. Julia was in the process of grabbing the African witch from behind when the latter swiftly turned and struck her with her broom on the face, while simultaneously running towards one of the windows and trying to fly away.

But Mirko wasn't going to let the witch escape. He instantly rushed forward and assailed her with a fierce blow to her chin. She fell and the others quickly pinned her to the ground: "You 're going nowhere. It's no use running when you're on a lonely road!" said Uwe, as they led her away, her hands firmly held behind her back.

As another contingent of the Hexenburg team pursued Toyosi, he deftly manoeuvred through the maze of towering shelves in the vast warehouse, evading their grasp with remarkable agility. Despite his small stature, Toyosi moved with surprising speed, seemingly slipping through their fingers like a slippery fish, his previously protruding belly now mysteriously absent. Meanwhile, inside the bag, Jenny tumbled about, her confinement becoming increasingly chaotic.

Eventually, Toyosi emerged from the labyrinth of goods, finding himself back amidst the ongoing clash between Sabon-Gari and Martin. Seeking cover behind his master, who had Martin pinned to the ground, Toyosi awaited his opportunity. With Martin struggling beneath his grip, Sabon-Gari performed a chilling transformation, morphing his walking stick into a venomous snake. With calculated cruelty, he taunted Martin with the deadly reptile, its mouth agape as it slithered menacingly across the young wizard's face.

In a moment of dire peril, just as Sabon-Gari prepared to unleash the snake's deadly bite, the warehouse doors swung open with a resounding clank. Ursula and Karl-Heinz swooped in, their arrival marking a pivotal turn in the confrontation. With a swift motion of her magic wand, Ursula unleashed a torrent of dazzling light, striking the snake, and saving Martin from its lethal fangs.

As the snake writhed in agony on the ground, Sabon-Gari released his grip on Martin, his attention swiftly turning to Toyosi and the bag containing Jenny. With a swift incantation, he commanded the bag to leap from Toyosi's grasp into his own awaiting hands.

Meanwhile, Mathias, a keen-eyed member of the Hexenburg team, noticed Toyosi standing on a metal pedestal connected to one of the warehouse machines. Drawing from his limited knowledge from a previous encounter with the machine following his brief visit in the past to a family friend who worked in a small firm with a similar machine in Bremen, he reckoned the position was a perfect point to trap the diminutive African wizard and he decided to give it a go and astutely hit the machine's activation button.

In an almost comical twist, before the small man could react, he was wrapped up in polythene that was automatically produced by the swirling machine. He was stuck and unable to get out and was then taken captive by the members of the Hexenburg team.

Ursula's arrival and dramatic entry into the large warehouse caused a flurry of excitement and largely boosted the confidence of the Hexenburg team. She alighted from her magic carpet to confront the Weafric leader. Up until this moment, while the Hexenburg witches and wizards were still trying to set Jenny free from the grip of their foreign adversaries, one thing was ominously missing - Their reason for kidnapping Jenny.

"Why don't you speak with him to hand Jenny over without shedding blood." Karl-Heinz addressed Ursula. She nodded gently in the affirmative as she walked close to Sabon-Gari and the two eyed each other.

It was a dramatic scene as the leaders of two opposed worlds of witches and wizards came face to face for the first time. They walked around in front of each other with one sizing up the other in a tensed stare-down - There was something creepy about him, Ursula thought, as she looked directly into the wizard's fierce-looking eyes.

"Who are you?" she accosted him.

"I'm Sabon-Gari." replied the Weafric2w leader after a little pause.

"And what is your mission here in our territory?" Ursula inquired.

"We're messengers from the other side and we're here on tour," answered Sabon-Gari.

"Do you have our daughter, Jenny, in your possession?" asked Ursula.

"Why are you questioning me? Am I your daughter's keeper?" replied the African wizard. The coldness in his voice coupled with the ferocious demeanour about him did not surprise or deter Ursula.

"I'm asking you because we have good reasons to believe that you have Jenny in your possession. Why have you abducted her?" she asked.

"Abducted her?" answered Sabon-Gari, bursting into a wild, fiendish laughter. Ursula momentarily looked into his eyes, and she could see something sinister in them.

"You've gone beyond your jurisdiction, and I hope you are aware that this is against the rules of the Federation; I want you to understand that you're fighting a losing battle and taking your colleagues on a wrong path." Said Ursula. "We don't want anybody to get hurt because of some deluded nuts. Now, all you can do is to let Jenny go." Ursula entreated.

"Are you accusing and threatening me without any evidence?" asked Sabon Gari, with a sly, calculating grin. He had a furtive look about him.

"I am not just accusing you, black wizard, but we know you have her." Replied the witch with an air of definitiveness. Ursula's diplomatic outreach seemed to have met a brick wall in the Weafric2w leader, and it had become apparent to her that this man would not let Jenny go without a fight and the battle line was drawn!

At that point, Ursula, sensing that the African wizard was not someone they could negotiate with, gestured to Karl-Heinz who then reached for the box lying on the magic carpet that was suspended in mid-air just above the ground. He opened the box and brought out a sword. It was a potent weapon whose blade had been specially treated.

"Ulla, these rogues are not getting away with this; Do this for Jenny." said Karl-Heinz while presenting the Hexenburg witches" leader with the sword.

Then, Ursula turned towards Sabon-Gari looking him in the eyes. "You have murdered sleep. Those looking for trouble will surely find it!" she said levelly.

On seeing her sword, Sabon-Gari suddenly burst into cryptic laughter, and just as quickly, his laughter gave way to a fierce look.

"You don't cut down an Iroko tree with a machete!" growled the Weafric2w leader with the aplomb of an experienced guest. The occult master subsequently, reached in his pocket and brought out a black handkerchief and held it out with outstretched arms towards the open window of the warehouse.

"He who shakes the iroko tree, shakes himself! Kubwa mlinzi! Mimi, mtumishi wako, piga juu yenu ! Chaubun-nagun-gamugg!" the fiery African sorcerer recited the spell, his voice throaty and penetrating.

In that pivotal moment, Sabon-Gari's countenance contorted in a grotesque display of transformation. His features twisted and distorted as spasms wracked his entire body. Strands of his hair writhed and squirmed, morphing into sinuous snakes with supernatural fluidity. The eerie sight transformed him into a nightmarish figure straight out of medieval lore, casting an ominous pall over the onlookers and eliciting shivers of dread.

As the unsettling metamorphosis unfolded, Sabon-Gari's handkerchief erupted into a sudden plume of smoke, a manifestation of his mystical prowess. With a flourish, he conjured a gleaming sword into his grasp, its razor-sharp edge slicing through the air with ominous intent. The mesmerized spectators watched with bated breath; their nerves frayed by the eerie spectacle. Some, overcome with fear, hastily sought refuge from the unfolding spectacle, their hearts pounding with trepidation.

"What an odious man! Ulla, go, get this damned horrible piece of work!" said Karl-Heinz, his cold and fierce eyes glaring at Sabon-Gari.

Then Ursula, who was carrying the weight of the Hexenburg expectation stepped forward with her sword drawn to confront the Weafric2w leader - It was the clash of two worlds. Then, with a grim sense of inevitability, the two came head-to-head squared off as they engaged in combat. The fighting was fierce as the long blades of their swords clashed. The African sorcerer was ready to fight to the death rather than let Jenny go. The pint-sized teenager in the little box screamed and her eyes gleamed as she whimpered and rolled from side to side in the little box while the fighting was going on.

Sabon-Gari soon got Ursula in a corner and dashed towards her with his sword pointed in her direction, but she quickly jumped and somersaulted out of harm's way. The Weafric2w leader was somewhat surprised at his opponent's guile, physicality, and amazing back-flipping stunts - she was unbelievably courageous for a woman!

Karl-Heinz saw the gleam of Ursula's sword against the light as it flashed through the air; The Hexenburg witches' leader fought back with grim determination, constantly mounting attacks on Sabon-Gari, while at the same time gallantly fighting herself out of danger whenever she found herself in a difficult situation. The atmosphere in the warehouse vibrated with tension as the team of Hexenburg witches and wizards, anxiety edged on their faces, urged their leader on. She was up to the task knowing that her opponent needed just one strike of the specially treated sword to end his life.

Amid the tense situation, two of the firm's line leaders arrived at the scene of the noisy and violent brawl.

"What in the world is happening here? And who are these people?" one of them cried over the hubbub and scene of absolute mayhem. On closer observation, the bosses realized that the combatants as well as many in the crowd who were carrying brooms were not part of the firm.

"Call the police!" The boss ordered.

At that moment, Ursula was on the offensive and the momentary spell of sustained pressure from her was only rebuffed by some desperate defending by Sabon-Gari. That was, however, to change when like an arrow from a bow, the Weafric2w leader streaked down Ursula's left side and lashed out a kick to her side and a punch to her chin that sent her crashing on the pile of wooden pallets in a corner.

And then, like a bear with a sour head, Sabon-Gari growled menacingly and with incoherent rage rushed towards Ursula who was lying on the pallets and aiming to strike her with his sword. But the witch instinctively moved her body from her position and drifting cleverly out of danger, raised her sword in the direction of the onrushing cagey African sorcerer who inadvertently ran into and impaled himself on the pointed end of Ursula's virulent, wickedly sharp, well-positioned sword that pierced through her rival's stomach and protruded from his back; He shrieked from the impact of the death stroke. The unexpected lethal blow was enough to break his resilience.

For a while, as he staggered in pain holding the bag containing the box and the USB sticks close to his stomach with one hand as if his life depended on it and his sword loosely in the other and facing the grim inevitability of death, the African sorcerer looked like he'd conjure a magic to overcome the effect of what he was presently going through.

The danger was not over yet, and Ursula was not done, she wanted to deal decisively with the tormentor-in-chief and the Hexenburg witches' leader proceeded to put him out of his misery. That very moment, she sighted a knife that was lying in a container beside her. The knife had a piece of paper with the words 'RESTMULL,' attached to it. She grabbed the knife and doing a double flip forward, she struck her foe in the heart, delivering a vicious blow that jolted him and his sword dropped from his hand.

Ursula hurried towards him and quickly wrenched the bag containing the little box from him. The Weafric2w leader tipped over the edge of the container fell inside the presser and got crushed by the running machine. His fate was sealed!

"Go to rack and ruin!" Ursula shouted at the dying African leader.

The Hexenburg team erupted in joy and celebration. They were glad that the bad African wizards and the witch had got their comeuppance. Almost immediately, the police arrived. Moments later, came the ambulance to cater for the injured.

"Ausweis, bitte?" said the police officer, addressing Toyosi.

"I ... I don't speak German." replied the small man, as panic engulfed the Africans' spirits.

"Ihren papiere, bitte ... Ihren ausweis?" repeated the officer.

Toyosi gnashed his teeth wistfully and stared at him with a look of apprehension written all over his face and could not understand what the officer was demanding; And Malaika rolled her eyes from side to side bemusedly and vacantly at the shocking turn of events, she was visibly overcome. That wasn't the kind of picture they had looked forward to when they set out and they looked on forlornly as the police led them away.

The paramount objective now was to free Jenny from the sinister enchantment that bound her and restore her to her true self. Ursula swiftly obtained permission from the authorities to seek aid from Lahm, her late father's trusted confidant in Osnabruck, in urgently breaking the curse that held Jenny in its grip.

Accompanied by a contingent of police officers, the Hexenburg team promptly made their way to Lahm's residence. With solemn reverence, Ursula carefully placed the box containing Jenny on her enchanted carpet within the spacious room. As she opened the box, Jenny, diminutive and silent, emerged from its confines, her presence evoking a mixture of concern and hope.

With gentle reassurance, Ursula guided Jenny out of the box and onto the magical carpet. Jenny's wide, innocent eyes scanned the faces around her, recognizing familiar figures amidst the assembly. A flicker of recognition danced across her features, culminating in a timid smile before she reclined on the carpet, which promptly levitated and carried her to a designated spot in the room.

Lahm, clad in a robe seemingly worn backwards to align with his peculiar stance, approached Jenny with deliberate steps, his feet turned in an unconventional direction. With a tender touch, he draped a silky blanket over Jenny's form, preparing to embark on the ritual to dispel the dark enchantment that ensnared her.

All attention was fixed on Jenny as Lahm initiated the ceremonial rites to purge her of the malevolent energies and dismantle the curse of the evil eye that plagued her. "Jenny, the power wielded by the one who cast this spell upon you has ceased with his demise," Lahm intoned solemnly, his words infused with ancient wisdom and mystical authority.

"From the domain of the secret –
From the corridor of the unspoken.
The guardians of the thirteenth world –
From the meeting point of two parallel lines.

I call upon you to redeem our dear daughter, Jenny!" Lahm's voice resonated through the room with solemn determination, each syllable infused with a potent blend of urgency and resolve.

Then, with deliberate grace, Lahm manoeuvred through the room, his feet tracing an unusual path as they pointed backwards in the opposite direction of his face, mirroring the arcane movements of his ancient rituals. He reached for his magic wand, a conduit for his mystical power, and held it aloft with reverent care.

Advancing towards Jenny, Lahm's movements defied conventional logic, each step a calculated dance between the realms of reality and the unseen. With a steady hand, he extended his wand towards the blanket enveloping Jenny, his touch imbued with a subtle energy that resonated through the fabric.

In a ritualistic gesture, Lahm invoked the sacred power of the wand, tracing intricate patterns through the air as he intoned the ancient incantations passed down through generations. Three deliberate taps upon the blanket catalysed the unseen forces of magic to awaken and converge upon Jenny, weaving a protective cocoon of mystical energies around her small fragile form.

"Jenny, I bid you, now, return to yourself!"
"Eta, Beta, ich flehe auch an - Verzaubern!"

In an instant, a delicate shroud of mist enveloped Jenny where she lay on the floor, obscuring her form from view. As the mist gradually dissipated, a remarkable sight unfolded before their eyes: Jenny, restored to her full size, rose gracefully from the dissipating haze that once veiled her.

A collective sigh of relief swept through the room, mingling with murmurs of astonishment from the police officers and onlookers who bore witness to the miraculous transformation.

"Jenny!" cried Petra.

"Mama!" exclaimed Jenny, as she ran with outstretched arms into her mother's warm embrace.

Jenny basked in the newfound tranquillity that enveloped her, a stark contrast to the harrowing ordeal she had endured. Petra, her mother, was overwhelmed with emotion, her eyes glistening with tears of relief. The past days had been a tumultuous roller-coaster for the entire family, and seeing Jenny safe brought an immense sense of solace.

Dieter, Jenny's father, couldn't contain his relief, his tense features softening into a smile. "It's finally over," he murmured, a weight lifted from his shoulders.

Petra, still processing the surreal events, turned to Ursula and Karl-Heinz with gratitude shining in her eyes. "I can't believe what we've been through. It felt like we were living in a horror movie," she confessed, her voice trembling with emotion. Addressing the assembled crowd, she continued, "True witches, like Ursula and Karl-Heinz, use their powers for good. Thank you all for standing with us, for fighting against the darkness."

Karl-Heinz nodded solemnly, his grip tightening on the bag containing the USB sticks, evidence of the nefarious activities that had threatened their family. "It was indeed an extraordinary situation," he agreed, his expression reflecting a mixture of relief and lingering tension. "But we're grateful it's come to an end. It could have been much worse," he added, exhaling deeply.

Lahm, the enigmatic wizard, couldn't help but chuckle at the turn of events, a hint of amusement dancing in his eyes amidst the seriousness of the moment.

Then Ursula, positively beaming with pleasure, placed her hand on Jenny's shoulder and addressed the crowd.

"I salute your courage and bravery! By your actions, you have all shown great promise for the future of our craft." And then, raising her voice, she said, 'What is our first code?'

"To show love and support for one another...always!" the members of the Hexenburg team responded in unison and busted into spontaneous applause.

The two police officers were puzzled by what they had just witnessed in the room that seemed to involve mysterious forces. And then, one of the officers addressed Ursula,

"I have to say that this is an extraordinary and bizarre case. However, you will have to come with us to the station to give a statement.

The Hexenburg School of Witches continued its mission of educating and training young witches and wizards, guided by dedicated teachers like Petra, who imparted their knowledge and passion for magic to the next generation. With each passing day, the students at the school grew in their understanding and mastery of witchcraft, inspired by the magical experiences and teachings they received within its walls.